The People on the Hill

The People on the Hill

A RED BADGE NOVEL OF SUSPENSE

by Velda Johnston

DODD, MEAD & COMPANY · *New York*

Johnston

ISBN 0-396-06281-4
Library of Congress Catalog Card Number: 71-134320
Printed in the United States of America
by Vail-Ballou Press, Inc., Binghamton, N.Y.

For my friends on the hill,
who aren't in the least like the people in this book.

1

Even from the foot of the low hill, Karen sensed that there was something odd, something subtly altered, about the people standing in a little group near the crest, their winter-clad figures dark against the snow.

One of them moved slightly, and his hair, like a smooth, pale blond cap, caught the greenish light of a nearby standard lamp. Her heart seemed to swell. David! But despite her eagerness to be with him, after almost two months away from New York, she still hesitated, feeling puzzled and even, inexplicably, a little chilled.

Certainly their dogs, the reasons for these nightly gatherings in Central Park, hadn't changed. They were as lively as ever. Three of them—May Cosgrove's crossbreed, Paul Winship's Airedale, and the Kinsings' big brown poodle—chased each other with mock ferocity, raising a cloud of snow particles which seemed to hang for a moment, iridescent in the lamplight, before settling back. Too dignified for such antics, David Bryant's Great Dane, Britt, sat over near the Metropolitan Museum's northern wall, watching them.

Suddenly Karen realized what had struck her as changed about her friends. They were so quiet. Always before there'd been a good deal of laughter and moving about and stick-throwing for the dogs. Now they stood motionless, and their voices came to her only as a subdued murmur.

The previous September, when she'd first started coming to the park with her near-collie, Bozo, she'd been pleased and flattered that the small group of regulars meeting on the hill had accepted her. Although a diverse group, with little in common except dog ownership and eastside residences, they'd often created an almost partylike atmosphere for half an hour or so each evening.

That was mainly David's doing, of course. With his charm and good looks and talent, David Bryant could have sparked almost any group into gaiety. It was David who, as a gag, had brought champagne and paper cups to the hill one November night, so that they could drink a birthday toast to his half sister, Consuelo Bryant. It was David, too, who'd proposed that they write to the Mayor, describing their party as an effort to cooperate with his campaign to take the park away from the hoodlums and criminals, and give it back to law-abiding New Yorkers. They'd stood around in the early dark, sipping champagne and giggling over each other's suggestions for the proposed letter. At last Karen, standing close to the standard lamp, had made a shorthand draft on the back of an old envelope. The typed communication, signed by all of them the next night, had been sent to the Mayor, who eventually had replied in the same mock-serious vein, thanking them for their efforts and reminding them to leave the empties in the litter basket.

Later, they'd drunk champagne on the hill for Henry Maize, a quiet-mannered insurance claims adjustor in his late fifties, and still later for Paul Winship, a necktie salesman, would-be song writer, and the only one of the group Karen didn't like. Karen herself was to have been honored in mid-December, but by then her father's illness had called her back to North Carolina.

Yes, those had been lively little gatherings. Why did they stand up there now so quietly, almost like people talking in subdued tones after a funeral?

A funeral. An association of ideas made her look uneasily

to her left, toward the museum parking lot. A girl had died there. It had happened about a month ago, although Karen had learned of it only within the last half hour from her landlady. Meeting Karen and her dog in the lower hall of the converted brownstone on Eighty-fourth Street, the landlady had warned, "Don't you take a step into the park unless you can see your friends up on the hill. Terrible things have happened in that part of the park while you were away. An old man was shot to death in that field where the kids play ball. And early in January a young girl was stabbed to death in the museum's north parking lot. The police think it happened around midnight."

Now the few cars standing in the lot were bathed in light streaming from one of the museum's ground-floor windows. It was easy to imagine, though, how dark and deserted the area had been on that January midnight. Karen wondered if the girl had wandered in there by herself or had arranged to meet someone. In either case, she must have been drunk or drugged or insane. No girl in her right mind would venture even that far into the park late at night.

Had something else happened, even more recently? Something that had hushed the voices and banished the laughter of that group on the hill?

Nonsense, she decided. At even the liveliest gatherings there are moments when people talk quietly, or not at all. Bending, she unsnapped Bozo's leash. Instantly he began to scramble up the hill through the snow, only to stop short and then roll abjectly on his back as Sistie, one of the three frolicking dogs, left the group and advanced upon him, stiff-legged.

Sistie was living refutation of the idea that a dog's personality always reflects that of its owner. A black and tan crossbreed of no distinction discernible to human eyes, Sistie was undisputed ruler of the dogs brought to the hill each night. At her demand, and after only token resistance, any dog would surrender to her the half-eaten salami sandwich

3

he'd found in the bushes. Of some dogs, such as Bozo, she demanded the ultimate gesture of submission—the limply raised paws, the meekly bared throat.

By contrast Sistie's owner, May Cosgrove, was a fey and gentle widow of around seventy, with an abiding enthusiasm for Hinduism, astrology, and other mystical doctrines, and a face so serene that it was impossible to imagine it contorted with anger.

Moving up the hill, her booted feet crunching through the thin crust, Karen saw Bozo get to his feet and trot beside Sistie toward the group of people. One of the women— Karen wasn't sure which—exclaimed, "Why, there's Bozo."

The faces had turned toward Karen now, watching her progress up the hill. Fleetingly she noticed that all seven of the "regulars" were there. But Karen, feeling a blend of eagerness, anxiety, and, at this last moment, an odd shyness, knew that David was the only one who mattered—David, who almost surely loved her, and yet hadn't written or phoned during her last three weeks down in North Carolina.

Because of those silent weeks, she found herself afraid to look at him directly, lest she read in his gray eyes a change in his feeling for her. But she was aware in every nerve of him standing there, several inches taller than even his tall and homely half sister, and with his pale blond hair gleaming in the lamplight.

She called out, "Hello, everybody."

For a moment no one replied. Then Doris Kinsing, standing short and rather plump beside her husband's tall bulk, answered, "Why, hello, stranger."

Her voice had held an edge. But then, that wasn't unusual. Doris Kinsing often sounded peevish. A still pretty brunette in her mid forties, Doris was, by her own account, a perennial victim of rude taxi drivers, incompetent salesgirls, and, in wet weather, motorists who deliberately splashed her with mud. As David had once said to Karen, "Doris Kinsing goes through life sending steaks back to the chef."

4

But she'd been reasonably cordial to Karen. In fact, Karen and David had gone to dinner at the Kinsings' apartment, and even though Karen hadn't enjoyed the evening—Doris had asked some disconcertingly personal questions—she'd regarded the invitation as evidence of Doris's friendly feelings for her. Now, though, the lack of welcome in the older woman's face was so apparent that Karen felt her own smile stiffen and die.

Standing beside her brother David, Consuelo Bryant asked, "Your father all right?"

"He's much better, thank you. His left leg is still partially paralyzed, but that will go away. He thinks he can resume his practice soon."

"I see."

Was Consuelo's manner, Karen wondered, even more abrupt than usual, or did she just imagine it? A dozen years older than David, Consuelo seemed so completely the spinster of legend and corny old jokes that one might have suspected her of self-caricature. Her clothing, especially when she came to the hill, was eccentric. Tonight she'd dressed her tall and rawboned body in dark wool pants and a man's sheepskin-lined canvas jacket. Topping her large, olive-skinned features was a wildly unbecoming hat, a knit jersey tam-o'-shanter covered with multi-colored plastic disks. Her manner was usually tart and a shade prim, although after two paper cups of champagne—and this, too, was often an element in the cruel legends and jokes—she became surprisingly bawdy, eliciting from David looks of slightly pained amusement.

In one respect, though, Consuelo didn't fit the spinster stereotype. She kept no cat, dog, or any other sort of pet. Obviously she came to the hill almost every night just to share her brother David's company for half an hour or so.

David, Karen thought. Why hadn't he spoken to her, moved to her side? She found courage to look at him. "Hello, David. How've you been?"

He smiled pleasantly, casually. "Oh, you know what they say about the wicked. I've flourished as the green bay tree. When did you get back to town?"

"This morning." She'd tried to phone him at his apartment. Twice the line had been busy, and the third time there'd been no answer.

"Well, too bad you had to leave balmy Ca'lina for old Sinus City."

Too bad. Too *bad!* She was aware of faint nausea, almost as if from an unexpected blow in the pit of her stomach.

She stood there, trying to hide her bewildered pain with a smile that felt nailed on. In a corner of her mind not completely taken up with David, she was aware that the others, too, were showing her little or no cordiality. The claims adjustor, Henry Maize, quiet, widowed Henry, whom she'd always liked, asked her in a constrained voice if she had the same apartment. She said yes. George Kinsing, Doris's tall, overweight husband, asked with equal constraint if she'd gotten her secretarial job back with that educational film company. Again she answered yes. As for the necktie salesman and would-be song writer, Paul Winship—tall, thin, thirty-eight, and wearing an overcoat he must have bought in a department store College Shop—he merely nodded to her and then resumed contemplation of the toes of his suede chukker boots. Usually Paul had been the most vocal of the group, telling malicious stories about his customers, and sprinkling his talk with hipster-musician slang that real musicians had stopped using years before.

Only little old May Cosgrove, that devotee of exotic religions, seemed unchanged. She said, patting her Sistie's rough head, "I'm glad your father is going to be all right, dear. Doctors are so important to the world." She straightened. "But then, I knew he'd be all right. Didn't you once tell me he was a Capricorn? Capricorns almost always have strong constitutions."

Light from the standard lamp glittered on Mrs. Cosgrove's

6

glasses, so that Karen couldn't see the expression in her eyes. But the smiling face with its halo of white sausage curls looked as gentle as ever. "Just the same," Mrs. Cosgrove added, "I prayed for him."

She didn't say to whom. Karen answered, "Thank you, Mrs. Cosgrove."

After that, silence settled down. In her puzzled hurt, Karen began to wonder if someone could have circulated ugly stories about her. Could David—? Oh, no. Even if his feelings toward her had changed, he wouldn't do that. Only little-minded, insecure men revenged themselves by slandering girls who refused to go to bed with them. And David, with his looks and talent and growing fame, had no reason to feel insecure. Besides, he'd accepted her refusal cheerfully and gone right on seeing her.

Nevertheless, she could sense their rejection of her, their desire for her to leave, almost as clearly as if they'd put it into words. At last, unable to bear it any longer, she turned and called, "Here, Bozo." The rough-coated dog, rooting at the foot of a leafless bush for bread left by some bird lover, turned and trotted to her. He had a blob of snow on his nose, and, as usual, his grin stretched from his one erect ear to the one he carried at permanent half mast. She snapped his leash to his collar. In a clear voice that shook only a little, she said, "Well, good night, everybody."

"Leaving?" David said. "I'll go with you."

Her pain and humiliation vanished under a flood of relief. What did it matter that the others seemed unfriendly? David, as usual, was going to walk home with her. And on the way, of course, he'd suggest that they have dinner together. David, she knew, prided himself on his cool. Probably he hadn't wanted to display his feelings until they were alone. Yes, surely that was it.

He fastened the Great Dane's leash. With a happy sense of the familiar, Karen moved beside David down the hill. As they passed the museum parking lot, now almost empty of cars, the thought of that girl brushed her mind. (Had there been enough light for her to see the face of her assailant, and perhaps the gleam of the upraised knife? Or had death come as a mercifully swift surprise?) Karen thrust the questions away from her. Now that David walked beside her, she didn't want to be aware that in New York almost anyone—a tired office worker waiting for a bus, an old lady fumbling for her key in an apartment house foyer, a girl sunning herself on a rooftop—could find himself facing the leveled gun, the unsheathed knife, or know an instant of surprise as the blow descended from behind. With David beside her, she wanted to think only of his New York, that city of handsome, successful, or about-to-be-successful people, of winter weekends in Vermont and summer weekends in the Hamptons, of bright, amusing talk in bars, theater lobbies, and in lines outside Third Avenue movie houses.

With a return of anxiety, she realized that David hadn't spoken yet. Then, just before they reached the traffic light, showing red, on the corner of Fifth Avenue and Eighty-fourth, he asked, "Have any trouble getting your job back?"

"No. I called Mr. Bokarski as soon as my plane got into Kennedy this morning, and he said to come to work tomorrow."

In fact Jan Bokarski, a Polish refugee, had been overjoyed to hear her voice. As he'd told her sorrowfully when she left New York, she was the only secretary he'd had in three years who'd been able to understand his accent. Karen, too, was pleased to be returning to Bokarski Films. She'd liked her job, which often involved accompanying a camera crew to such varied locations as a New Jersey oil refinery belching fumes and a sullen red glare, and the transplanted medieval monastery up the Hudson, with its agonized thirteenth-century statues of martyred saints and its courtyard flagstones worn hollow by the sandaled feet of monks long dead.

The light changed. As they moved across Fifth Avenue, she asked, "How is your work going?"

"Not bad. I've been asked to do the theme music for a new TV series they'll be making out in Hollywood, when and if they get the financing."

"That's good."

He didn't answer. As they moved along the broad sidewalk, with the dogs trotting ahead, she felt her exaltation of a few minutes before drain completely away. Something was wrong, definitely wrong. But they'd crossed Park Avenue before she found the courage to ask, "Why were you all so different tonight?"

"Different?"

"So—standoffish."

He smiled down at her. "Seems to me you were pretty standoffish yourself. I thought you were never going to speak to me."

"I—I guess I felt a little scared, or shy, or—"

She broke off, realizing that both her words and her tone must have told him how her feeling for him had grown during these weeks of absence, and how her heart had swelled tonight at her first glimpse of his pale blond head. Well, she thought, her pulses racing, perhaps that was all to the good. Perhaps now he'd drop this tormenting, offhand manner of his, and turn to her reassuringly, tenderly.

He said, "Shy? You reverted, that's what. You were well on your way to developing New York cool. Then you went back to the land of black-eyed peas—or do they eat black-eyed peas in North Carolina?"

So he hadn't understood. Or, if he had, he'd chosen to pretend he hadn't. She didn't even try to think up an amusing reply. She said in a flat voice, "Some people do."

Neither of them spoke again until they reached Lexington Avenue. Then he stopped and looked down at her. Light spilling from a corner restaurant showed his face clearly—the pale hair brushed low across his broad forehead, the gray eyes with the fine lines at the corners that came partly from squinting at the sun on ski slopes and partly from being

9

thirty, the even but strong features, the flashing smile.

"Sorry I can't walk you the rest of the way home, but I'd better get back to my own pad. If I don't make out some checks tonight, I'll have bill collectors knocking at my door."

She said, in the voice of a polite child who's just been told to go home because the party is over, "Well, good night."

For a moment she gazed after him as, with Britt, he strode toward his Eighty-second Street apartment. Then she looked down at Bozo. He sat there on the curb, grinning up at her. She asked, "What's so funny?"

At the sharpness of her tone, he closed his mouth and slid his paws forward until he lay on the sidewalk, rolling puzzled and aggrieved eyes up at her. A briefcase-carrying man stepped over him without breaking stride and hurried on.

She felt compunction. It was wrong to resent Bozo's cheerful heart, just because her own was filled with pain. "Come on," she said, tugging at his leash. "Let's go home."

2

With their brown standard poodle straining at the leash, George and Doris Kinsing turned north on Fifth Avenue toward their Eighty-ninth Street apartment. Doris said, "That girl! I hoped we'd seen the last of her."

For all their sakes, George had hoped so, too. And yet it had been a pleasure to see the little Wentworth girl tonight. She'd looked so pretty, with those long-lashed hazel eyes of hers, and a strand of brown hair showing beneath the rabbit's fur hood that framed her delicate face. What in other faces might have seemed flaws—the slightness of her chin, the light dusting of freckles across her straight little nose— only made her more appealing. Yes, she'd looked pretty— and puzzled and hurt.

His wife said, "I was so sure David was going to snub her. But what does he do? He walks off with her!"

Her husband's side glance held sadness and a kind of wry, weary amusement. David was far from being the first young man she'd fallen in love with. Eight or nine years ago there'd been that man who played "cocktail piano" in the afternoons at a bar on lower Fifth Avenue. Together with a divorcee friend of hers—it was ostensibly the divorcee who had a "crush" on Roger, or Ron, or whatever his name was —Doris would spend three or four afternoons a week at the bar. Often George himself had reached the apartment before she came home, flushed and bright-eyed and smelling of gin.

Several years later there'd been the manager of a Madison Avenue bookshop. For a couple of months Doris, who seldom read anything but fashion magazines, brought home books with titles like *Freud and Marx: An Attempt at Synthesis* or *Aspects of Objectivism*.

Like anyone in love, Doris had been unable to resist speaking the beloved's name, and so she'd chattered to George about Roger—or Ron—and about Max. Yes, that was the bookshop manager's name. Max. But it was the pianist's "talent" she'd spoken of, and Max's "intellect." Just what her relations with either of them had been, he didn't know. Nor had it mattered.

But the consequences of her present infatuation mattered. They mattered crucially. Had she grasped that? Did she actually realize that by their silence they'd made themselves accessories to a criminal act, and that each day that passed increased their complicity?

Moving toward the curb with a cab whistle in his hand, a doorman near the corner of Eighty-sixth Street said to the Kinsings, "Good evening, madam. Good evening, sir," and George answered, "Good evening." For almost every night of the seven years since they'd acquired Henri, the poodle, they'd exchanged greetings with that particular doorman. They didn't know his name, and probably never would. New York, George thought.

When they'd crossed the intersection, Doris said, "I can't imagine what David was thinking of! If Karen had ever meant anything to him, perhaps I could understand it, but I'm sure she never did."

"No," George thought, "you aren't sure at all." It was because she wasn't sure that she'd asked David and Karen to dinner one night about a week before the girl had been called home to North Carolina. George had wondered at the invitation, but after dinner, while they had coffee in the living room, all had become clear. Obviously trying to learn the nature of their relationship, Doris had put both young people on the grill. Were girls of Karen's age as—well, free as people said? And that weekend when they'd gone skiing in Stowe. Where had they stayed?

David had fielded her questions easily, banteringly, his gray eyes holding an amused shine. But George had felt sorry for the little Wentworth girl, trying to hide her embarrassed resentment, trying to answer politely. And he'd felt even sorrier for Doris, asking her clumsy, outrageous questions.

He glanced down at his wife's profile, with its pert nose, short upper lip, and firm chin. Had he ever been in love with her? Perhaps. She was pretty still, and she'd been even prettier in those days right after World War Two. George had been pleased and proud that such a pretty girl was willing to have an affair with him, just as he'd been proud that he, a bookkeeper trained under the G.I. Bill of Rights, had found a job at the munificent salary of five hundred a month.

He hadn't intended to marry her, at least not as soon as he did. Not that it was a shotgun wedding. Her parents, a quiet Staten Island couple, hadn't been the shotgun-toting type. But after a few months he became aware, without realizing how it happened, that certain assumptions had been made. By Doris, and all of her friends. By her parents. By his parents, who'd come down from Albany to see their son, with his good job, and his girl who'd turned out to be just as pretty and sweet as his letters had said she was.

And so, on a May afternoon, he'd stood before the altar of a Staten Island church, with his bride beside him and a sense of doom weighting his heart. Perhaps, he told himself, many now happily married people had felt like this at their weddings. Perhaps millions of men, and women, too, had heard, like a counterpoint to the minister's familiar and solemn words, an inner voice saying, "It's a mistake, a mistake, a mistake."

The first weeks of their marriage hadn't been so bad. Even though Doris had left her typist's job, they could still afford, in those days of the unshrunken dollar, a sizable one-bedroom apartment on Eighty-ninth Street, just off Fifth Avenue. Doris proved to be an immaculate housekeeper and an adequate, if unimaginative, cook. But from the first she manifested wide swings in mood, some evenings apparently sunk in depression, other evenings demanding with feverish gaiety that they "go out on the town, not sit here like old married sticks." Perhaps most women were like that, George told himself. And perhaps most wives believed their account of a visit to a hairdresser's that afternoon, or of a movie they'd seen, would hold their husbands enthralled. Besides, in fairness he had to recognize that it wasn't her intellect that had attracted him to her.

It took George several months to realize that she was more than a moody person, more than just an often boring chatterbox. She was a chronic collector of injustices. Almost every day, it seemed to George, Doris encountered something or someone who outraged her. Sometimes, as he watched his wife's face flush and her pale blue eyes grow bright as she recounted how she'd "told off" a butcher she was sure had tried to cheat her, or a bus driver who'd deliberately started up before she was seated, the chilling word "paranoia" would cross George's mind.

He began to take martinis—at first just one, later on two, or even two and a half—before dinner each night. After dinner—sometimes while he watched the screen of their newly acquired TV set, but more often while he read a book on the stock market or accounting—he'd consume several gin-and-tonics. At first Doris had protested, but after a while she ceased to comment on his drinking. Sometimes he'd look up from his book to find her watching him with an odd, shrewd expression in her light blue eyes. At such moments he felt he could almost read her thoughts. The drinks kept him soothed and at home. Besides, he was, in the classic phrase, a good provider. And so, just as long as he didn't drink himself out of his job—

They'd been married almost five years when George began to think seriously of a divorce. At this stage of their lives, they could easily go their separate ways. He was only thirty-one, and Doris not yet twenty-five. True, he'd have to pay alimony until she remarried. But anything would be better than this, dulling himself with booze each night to the boredom and emptiness of his marriage.

He'd almost mustered up enough courage to broach the subject of divorce when, one night, she told him that she thought she was pregnant. Three days later a doctor confirmed her surmise.

George did his best to fight off a sense of prison doors clanging shut. It wasn't fair to his future son or daughter, he told himself, that he should rebel against the child's very existence. Besides, parenthood might change both of them. Perhaps it was only her childless idleness that had made Doris seem so shallow, so prone to read deliberate malice into the small daily annoyances that most people took in their stride.

On New Year's Eve, with Doris already four months pregnant, they attended a celebration given by George's college fraternity. The party, a large and lavish one, was held in the Elks Hall of a town on Long Island's North Shore. Drinking with this brother and that brother, some of whom had been in college years before or years after he had, he suddenly realized that he was very drunk—drunker than he'd ever been in public since his army days. "Fresh air," he thought. He didn't even look around for Doris. Minutes before—or was it nearer an hour?—he'd seen her laughing with a group of celebrants, most of them male, at one of the tables. Aware that he staggered, he moved through swinging glass doors to the stone veranda above a long flight of stairs leading down to the parking lot.

He'd started down the steps when he realized that Doris

was beside him, her voice shrill with justifiable rage. He heard the phrase "spectacle of yourself," and "not fit to drive home." Then his foot slipped. In his drunkenness he must have grabbed her arm for support, because they both fell, tumbling down the long flight of steps to land at the foot, with his body lying heavily across hers. He heard one sharp scream of pain, and then mingled moans and sobs. Even before two men running down the steps had reached them, George had got to his feet, suddenly and bleakly sober. He'd thought, "I've killed him. I've killed my own child."

At the hospital the next day, he learned that more than an unborn child had been lost. The nature of his wife's injuries were such that an immediate operation had been necessary. Doris would never conceive again. Walking from the hospital, George Kinsing knew that he'd had his last drink. He also knew that in death their unborn child had bound him more closely to Doris than it could have if it had lived.

Toward the end of her third week in the hospital, when she was well on the way to recovery, Doris accused her nurse of poisoning her. The nurse's denial had brought on a rage so violent that the use of a sedative became necessary.

A few days later, one of her doctors told George the result of a consultation with a psychiatrist. Mrs. Kinsing needed to be confined to a mental sanitarium.

As he sat there in an office on the hospital's third floor, the fingers of George's big hands had bitten into his knees. Was there to be no end to his guilt? "You mean that, from now on—"

"Of course not! She may be well in a matter of months. This sanitarium in Connecticut, the one that we recommend for her, has done wonderful things with chemical therapy. And it sometimes happens that an accident such as hers is followed by at least a mild psychosis, although usually it takes the form of melancholia. You see, a miscarriage is a profound emotional shock to a woman, as well as a physical one."

"If I suggest to her that we adopt a child—" He'd been thinking about that. Anything, anything to repair as much as possible the havoc he'd made.

"Out of the question!"

"I didn't mean now, or even soon. Eventually."

The doctor hesitated. "Mr. Kinsing, her miscarriage was the precipitating factor in your wife's present mental difficulty, but only that. From our observations, as well as from data you and her parents have given us, it's obvious that she's had paranoid tendencies for a long time, perhaps since childhood. We hope that after her recovery she'll stay well. But raising an adopted child might prove too much of a strain for her, even if you two could qualify now as adoptive parents, which I doubt. No, your wife's best chance is a life as free as possible from emotional stress."

"I see," George said.

In the twenty years that had passed since Doris, after a five months' stay, emerged from the sanitarium, George hadn't taken a drink. Work had been his opiate against quiet desperation. Attending night classes at Columbia, he'd earned his CPA. He'd been steadily promoted, and now was his firm's comptroller, with the title of vice president. Five years before, when the penthouse of their apartment building became available, the Kinsings had moved into it.

As for Doris, her behavior—despite her chronic complaints, despite her infatuations with men ten or more years younger than herself—had remained within bounds that could be considered normal. George made only mild attempts to talk her out of her grudges, and ignored her infatuations. As well as he could, he'd provided her with that unstressful life the doctor had recommended.

But now this appalling mess of David Bryant's, in which both he and Doris had become entangled . . .

Henri, the poodle, stopped to sniff a favorite fire hydrant. The Kinsings waited and then turned down Eighty-ninth Street.

As he had done so often these past weeks, George relived the first shock of that night. David, leaning against Henry Maize's middle-aged shoulder, his handsome face for once not self-assured, but white with fear. The appalled faces of the others. And the voice of Consuelo Bryant, David's sister, low in tone, and yet as urgent as if she's been shrieking.

"It was an accident. Do you hear? An accident! You've all got to give him at least twenty-four hours, so he can make up his mind what to do. Now promise!"

And each of them, for reasons which in a couple of cases George could only guess at, had promised.

Later that night, in their apartment, Doris had faced him with a wild, bright gleam in her eyes. "You've got to keep your promise. If you don't, if you smash David with this, I won't be able to stand it. Do you understand me?"

He'd understood. And he'd kept silent, not just for twenty-four hours, but ever since that night. So, apparently, had the others.

Now, walking beside his expensively dressed wife, with their expensive poodle straining at the leash, George wondered enviously at the moral certainty of others. Most people seemed sure of what acts were right and what wrong. Killing was wrong, and sheltering a killer—except in time of war, of course. And even in wartime, most people drew moral lines. Dropping bombs that might, and often did, kill infants in arms was so praiseworthy it might bring you a medal. But killing that same infant at close range with a gun or bayonet could bring you a court-martial.

There was no satiric edge to his thoughts. In his extremity, he honestly envied those who could split moral hairs with such calm sureness. He himself had no sureness at all. Was he wrong not to have gone to the police? Or was he right in trying to protect his wife—his absurd, pitiful wife,

18

made barren by him—from a shock that might send her back to what she always referred to as "that place"?

Herbert, the Jamaican who'd been night doorman of the apartment house almost as long as George and Doris had been its tenants, said, "Good evening, Mrs. Kinsing, Mr. Kinsing."

He looked after them approvingly as they walked back toward the elevator. A moralist as well as something of a snob, Herbert took a dim view of many people who'd moved into the apartment house in recent years. Those South Americans, for instance, some sort of U.N. delegates. And those three girls in 5-C, whose male guests sometimes didn't leave until daybreak. And that long-haired, bearded playwright in 11-E, whose wife went grocery shopping in blue jeans. Blue jeans! No, what Herbert liked were quiet, settled couples like the Kinsings.

3

Slumped low in a black leather armchair, David Bryant stared unseeingly at the dull gleam of a baby grand piano in the far corner of his living room. Damn it, why had Karen come back into his life just now?

Not that he didn't like her. He liked her very much. Thinking about her after she left for North Carolina, he'd decided that in almost every way Karen represented a balance between too much and too little. She was attractive, but not with that eye-blinding beauty which had turned some of the models and cover girls he'd known into narcissistic wrecks, esteeming themselves only for their looks, and so obsessed by those looks that an ounce of weight gained, or a facial blemish, could plunge them into acute anxiety. Karen was intelligent and apparently competent in a demanding job, but unlike some women he knew, her ambition wasn't strong enough to make her a candidate for ulcers. She knew and enjoyed music, and could even sight-read. Often he'd handed her a few bars of some recent composition of his across a restaurant table, and watched her face with pleasure as it responded to the music she was hearing in her mind. And yet she had neither the talent nor aspiration to become in any way his competitor.

She was well bred, too, not in that crisp Smith-Vassar-Wellesley sort of way, but with the gentler kind of manners which, apparently, some southern girls still absorbed. David liked that. In thinking about her after she left New York, he'd even found, somewhat to his surprise, that he liked her all the better for having refused to tumble into bed with him.

In short, he'd thought seriously of asking her to marry him. After all, he'd reached a good age for marriage, and he doubted that he'd ever find a girl who'd fit better into the sort of life he'd mapped out for himself. He might very well have gone down to North Carolina and proposed to her, if the sky hadn't fallen in on Chicken Little.

But fall it had. Oh my yes, it had.

Restless, he moved across the room and, at a small bar, mixed himself a Scotch-and-soda. He'd much have preferred marijuana. But the law, in its omniscience, permitted hangover-making booze, while forbidding mild, soothing grass. And it would be silly to risk even the hundred-to-one chance that some busybody neighbor, sniffing the air outside his door, would call the police here. That one visit from the police, the day after the accident—he'd trained himself to think of it as "the accident"—had been more than enough.

Glass in hand, he returned to the leather chair. His gaze, wandering to his tall bookcase, found the bronze statuette awarded him for the best musical score presented on television last year. Gloom settled over his face, drawing his features downward so that, in the light of the lamp beside his chair, he looked almost middle-aged. The next few years had promised to bring him so much. Flights to Hollywood— and London and Paris and Rome—to write motion picture scores. And money, lots of money, perhaps enough to buy a flat in Paris and a house in Marrakesh.

Well, it could still happen. In a few more weeks, after he became almost certain that the police had decided the accident would remain one more unsolved case, he'd light out for France or Italy. Even if the Hollywood people didn't raise the money for the new TV series, he could get by for at least a year, living off his residuals and the royalties from the one record album he'd made.

But for a little while longer, he mustn't draw attention to himself by leaving town. For a little longer he'd have to remain the prisoner of those six people. A prisoner of that ridiculous Paul Winship, with his ambitions of being a composer. A prisoner of that riggish—he liked Shakespeare's adjective for women like that—Doris Kinsing and that nutty May Cosgrove with her white sausage curls and her horoscopes. Twice since the accident, he'd felt it expedient to accept her invitation for "a chat at my little place." In her basement apartment, with steampipes knocking and gurgling overhead, she'd served him tea in a cup of heirloom china. Apparently she hadn't noticed that the cup, unused for the Lord only knew how long, had been coated with dust inside. Floating to the top, the dust had formed a fine scum on the tea's surface. He'd drunk the weak liquid and tried to register fascinated interest as she chattered on about Krishnamurti, and oversouls, and gurus.

Well, it would be worth it if those six, in Congressman Adam Clayton Powell's immortal words, kept the faith, baby. So far, obviously, they had.

How long would they stick by him? Well, in his sister Consuelo's case, until hell froze over. He was equally sure of poor, terrified Henry Maize, and almost sure of Paul Winship. Deep inside, the poor jerk must know he had no talent, that his only hope of leaping from behind Bloomingdale's tie counter into the gaudy success of his dreams was to have David tinker with those alleged songs of his. (Tinker, hell. David would have to take off the titles, run new music under them, and hope and pray he could get some publishing house to accept them. If that happened, Paul would still believe the songs were his, just because he wanted so desperately to believe that.)

He was fairly sure, too, that Doris Kinsing would stick with him, at least for a while. Once or twice in the past few weeks he'd thought of arranging to meet her some afternoon. A spot of hand-holding in some midtown bar might help ensure her silence. But he might have to keep it up, and sooner or later a woman that emotionally erratic was almost certain to take offense at something he did or failed to do. No, better to go on as he had, implying with a glance, a wry smile, and sometimes with a few low-toned, not-too-subtle words that if she weren't married, or if he didn't find her husband such a nice guy . . .

Her husband. That one David wasn't sure of. Why should a solid professional man like George Kinsing allow himself to be made a criminal accomplice for even twenty-four hours, let alone several weeks? Was he that blindly enamored of the overage wayward girl he was married to? Apparently, and thank God for it.

The last one, May Cosgrove, seemed to David the least dependable. What reason could a lady of her years—and she was a lady; she'd told him that before love had led her into a happy but financially straitened marriage, she'd been Miss May Vandering of the Philadelphia Main Line Vanderings—what reason could she have for helping him? He'd studied her behavior for some sign of senile passion for him, and had seen nothing but friendly concern. Friendliness, though, wasn't sufficient reason for standing by him. And yet she had. In fact, she was the one who, with a seraphic smile, had held out a neatly gloved hand and said, "Let me take it. I'll hide it so no one will ever find it." He remembered seeing the dull gleam of metal as he extended his hand toward hers.

The downstairs buzzer sounded. Setting down his drink, he moved across the room and unhooked the earpiece of the intercom beside the door. "Hello," he said into the little grille.

"It's me," Consuelo's voice said. "I'm coming up."

"Okay." He pushed the button that released the catch on the downstairs door and then replaced the earpiece, feeling irritation with the mechanism. Someday he'd live in a house with twenty-four-hour doorman and elevator service. He waited until he heard the elevator stop, and then opened the door.

With an abrupt nod, his sister strode past him and sat down in a straight chair. She'd exchanged her wool pants for a gray skirt, but she still wore the sheepskin jacket and that spangled thing on her dark hair. Poor Consuelo. What unhappy inspiration had led her mother to give her child a glamorous name? He didn't know. But until recently he'd been sure that his father's first wife must have been taking ugly pills before her daughter was born. He'd seen photographs of Consuelo's mother, and so knew that she'd been an attractive woman. Then about a year ago, soon after his father's death, he'd started rummaging through a trunkful of miscellaneous possessions, sent down to him from the old Bryant home in Maine. Among some tintypes he'd found one of a woman in a long dress with leg-o'-mutton sleeves. From under the brim of a boater, his half sister's face had stared grimly at the camera. Affixed to the back of the tintype was a sticker, bearing in his father's hand the information that this was a picture of his first wife's aunt. So that explained why Consuelo had missed out on the Bryant good looks, and her mother's, too. She was a throwback.

David said, "Drink?"

"You know I don't drink. Why do you always ask me that?"

"Force of habit, I guess." Sitting down in the leather chair, he lifted his glass and sloshed around the inch or so of pale liquid that remained.

"David, you were a damned fool tonight."

He didn't bother to fence with her. "You're wrong. If I hadn't walked Karen part of the way home, I'd have been a damn fool. She might have concluded there was something seriously wrong, with everybody giving her the cold shoulder. But I walked her to Lexington Avenue, all nice and friendly,

24

and left her there. Now she'll figure that although I'm willing to be friends, she just doesn't turn me on anymore. She'll be too busy thinking about that to puzzle her head about all of us. And she'll feel—well, too humiliated to join us in the park again."

Although Consuelo's tone was grudging, he saw a gleam of admiration in her eyes. "Maybe you're right. I do hope you won't miss her. Personally, I always considered her a mousy little thing."

You mean, David thought, that you kept hoping I'd consider her that. For a moment he amused himself by picturing how she'd look if he said, "Sister Mine, don't you feel that your excessive affection for Baby Brother is just a mite unseemly?" He'd never risk it, of course. She might forgive him, and then again she might not.

In the past, oppressed by her bullying affection, he'd often thought of trying to find her a husband. Henry Maize, say. Meek, frightened Henry would feel he had to do almost anything David asked of him. But now he was glad his sister was still single. Better, far better, that he remain the sole focus of her devotion.

The phone rang. Consuelo said, rising, "Go ahead and answer it. I was leaving anyway. I just dropped by on my way to the movies."

Crossing the room, he waited until the door closed behind her, and then lifted the phone from its cradle.

"David? Paul Winship here. I didn't get a chance to ask you at the park tonight, what with the Wentworth babe turning up, but anyway, have you had a chance to do anything about those songs of mine?"

"Quite a lot." That was more or less true. Using two bars of one song, he'd built it into what he hoped Paul would consider—sickening phrase—a catchy tune.

"Could we run the stuff over on my old upright some night soon?"

"Of course. How about Friday night?"

"Do you have to wait that long? I mean, are you free tomorrow night?"

A muscle along David's jaw leaped twice before he answered pleasantly, "I can make it tomorrow."

"Oh, fine. We'll come from the park straight to my place. I'll whip up a supper. I have a light hand with an omelet, if I do say so myself."

"Sounds great," David forced himself to say. "See you then," he added, and hung up.

After staring at the bar for a moment, he decided against having another drink. Oh, damn! It would be so nice to be sitting across a restaurant table from Karen right now. Those big hazel eyes of hers with the long lashes. Real ones. The genuineness of her response to his talk, even quite technical talk, about orchestrating music. When he used some term she didn't understand, she'd ask the definition and then nod her shiny brown head, almost visibly filing his words away in her memory.

Oh, to hell with it. Karen was out. If she caught even an inkling of the truth about him, she'd turn him in, no matter what pain it cost her. Morally speaking, Karen still saw the world in terms of black and white. At twenty-two, she was too young to realize that almost everything and everybody was gray. A dirty gray.

He turned to the record rack beside his hi-fi. The first LP he pulled out happened to be his own, featuring the theme music from a children's TV fantasy called *The Blue Planet*. It was this theme that had won him the bronze statuette atop his bookcase. He thrust the LP back, selected another, and put it on the turntable. With a staccato rattle of drums and a savage shriek of brasses, Khachaturian's "Dance of the Young Turks" cascaded from the loud-speakers.

4

In her darkened studio apartment, Karen lay staring at the shadow of the fire escape railing outside her window, cast on the opposite wall by a light in some window across the narrow courtyard. On the floor beside her bed, stretched out on his pallet, and perhaps chasing a dream rabbit over a dream landscape, Bozo made whining noises deep in his throat.

I'll get over it, she told herself. Of course she would. But it had been hard to take. He hadn't even tossed her a vague, face-saving, "Let's have dinner sometime soon." He'd just walked off.

Well, maybe he'd chosen the kinder way, at that. If he'd lost interest, as he obviously had, it was better that she know it right now.

Perhaps the loss of David wouldn't seem so devastating if she'd met other New York men who interested her. But she hadn't. Soon after she'd come to the city the previous June and taken a job with Bokarski Films, she'd started going out with the firm's only bachelor, a pleasant-mannered man of twenty-eight. On their fifth date he'd confided that he had two ex-wives. A man with that track record, she'd felt, shouldn't be encouraged. From then on she'd made excuses not to go out with him, until he'd finally stopped asking.

In late August, another girl at Bokarski Films had persuaded her to go to one of the dating bars on Second Avenue. Standing in line on the sidewalk outside the bar that hot Friday night, observing the false nonchalance of the other girls and the young men, and realizing that her own smile was too fixed and bright, she wondered what her parents—her gentle father, her garden-club-president mother—would think of their daughter now.

Almost as soon as she was in the place, standing at the long bar with a glass of beer cold and sweaty in her hand, a handsome, pleasant-voiced young man approached her. He introduced himself, commented on the crowded state of the room, and in the next breath asked if she were on the pill. Gathering up her purse and her dignity, she said, "Are there many more around like you? I hope not," and turned away.

But subsequently she did date two of the men who asked for her phone number that night. The first one, she discovered, was a science fiction fan. During dinner, he told her the plots of five stories in the current issue of *Cosmic Worlds*. Later on, at a banjo music place on Third Avenue, he recounted the plots of the remaining seven stories, his voice cutting through the music as persistently as a power saw. With green-haired men, berserk robots, and a slime that threatened to engulf the world swimming before her eyes, Karen asked herself, "Shall I tell him right now that I've got a splitting headache? Or shall I be a nice, polite girl and wait until midnight?"

The second young man had turned out to be locked in the throes of an identity crisis. All through their first and only date he brooded aloud and lovingly over his psyche, using words like "anomie" and "privatism," and asking her at intervals whether or not she thought he'd ever find himself. Hoping he would, but feeling reluctant to accompany him on that particular treasure hunt, she declined his request for another date.

Nor did she accept her office friend's suggestion that they

try another of the Second Avenue dating bars. With her luck, Karen felt, she might draw a Maoist the next time, who'd expect her to spend the evening making bombs.

In his sleep, Bozo gave a few strangled yips. His dream, evidently, had taken an ominous turn. Reaching down, she stroked his furry head until he fell silent.

It was through Bozo, she reflected, that her whole life in New York had changed.

She'd never even thought of acquiring a dog until the September afternoon when she came home to find a locksmith putting a new lock on her apartment door. Beside him stood her stout and motherly landlady, looking so agitated that Karen, who knew the woman had a heart condition, felt alarmed. "What's happening, Mrs. Orford?"

"I'm changing all the locks. And as soon as I can afford to, I'll put bars on your window, and every other window that opens onto that fire escape."

She told then how the elderly pensioner on the second floor, the only tenant beside Karen who lived alone, had been robbed sometime during the night. He'd awakened that morning to find both his wallet and his small portable TV set gone.

"And I think you should get a dog, Karen. It may be months and months before I can afford window bars, what with taxes and all. But if you had a dog, I wouldn't worry about you."

Chilled at the thought of a dark figure stepping over the window sill as she lay asleep, Karen said, "I suppose I should get one. But it would be cruel to leave a dog shut up by himself all day."

"You wouldn't have to. Your dog could stay in my apartment until you got home. I'd be glad of the company. And he can go out into the courtyard whenever he wants to."

Karen thought it over for a few days, and then went to the ASPCA, hoping to find a Yorkie or some other kind of

29

terrier. A small dog would fit more easily into her one-room-kitchenette apartment, and be cheaper to feed. But almost as soon as she started down the cement aisle, a collielike crossbreed with one rakishly drooping ear had moved to the bars of his cage and grinned at her.

Abandoning all thought of a small dog, she said, "Hello, Bozo, you clown, you."

She knew that she ought to think up some cleverer and more amusing name for him. But Bozo seemed to fit him so exactly that it stuck. It was as Bozo that he trotted ahead of her to the park that golden September evening, and scrambled up the low hill just north of the museum. Each of the little group of people up there, including the tall young man with the strikingly pale hair, had smiled at her with the easy camaraderie of dog owners. And when she and Bozo left the park, David Bryant and his Great Dane left with them.

Perhaps, she mused, it meant that she had a streak of what the feminists call Aunt Tomism, but it wasn't until she met David that New York seemed to become her city. With him beside her, it was all hers. The tall buildings, light-jeweled towers in the winter dusk, ringing Central Park's hills and meadows. The rink below Rockefeller Center's promenade, aswirl with brightly clad skaters on Sunday afternoons. The noise and glare of the theater district ten minutes before curtain time, and the quiet of certain side streets in the east seventies lined with houses of such last-century elegance that you almost expected some of Henry James's characters to emerge from the fanlighted doorways.

It wasn't until their fourth date that David had made the almost inevitable pass. Across a table in a midtown restaurant, he said, "Do you really want to see that movie? How about going to my place instead? We'll mix a drink, stack some records on the hi-fi—"

Miserable at the thought that this might be their last date, she said, "No, thanks. I'd rather see the movie."

He said, still smiling, "So I just don't turn you on."

"That's not it."

"What then? Could it possibly be that you're that phenomenon I've heard about, a twenty-two-year-old maiden who intends to stay that way until she's married? I advise you not to wait. What if you discover, in the bridal suite, that it was all a ghastly mistake?"

"I didn't say I'd wait until then."

He studied her for a moment. "I get it, perhaps. You intend to wait until you find someone you think you want to marry, and who thinks he wants to marry you."

"That's about it."

"Well," he said cheerfully, "at least we've got that cleared up. And now that we have, let's go to the movies."

All through the movie, she'd worried that he might not see her again. But with no change in his manner, he'd continued to take her out. And when in mid-December she'd been summoned home because of her father's stroke, David had called the airline to arrange for shipping Bozo in the plane's baggage compartment, and then had driven them both to the airport.

He'd sent her a book of Renoir reproductions for Christmas, plus a big box of her favorite candy, marzipan, from a little shop on Eighty-sixth Street. On New Year's Eve he'd telephoned, sounding far more warm and tender than he had at any time while she was still in New York. A week later he'd phoned again.

After that silence. No letters, no cards, no calls. More than once she'd been tempted to call him, but she'd felt that, particularly if he were absorbed in work, he might not like that. Besides, her father was on the mend. She'd be able to return to New York soon.

Well, she had returned, but not to David. David, plainly, was no longer interested.

One thing was certain. She'd go to the hill tomorrow night, and perhaps a few times after that. She'd go because her father had once said to her, "There's one thing that no one but yourself can take away from you, and that's your self-respect." Self-respect demanded that she show David, and the others, that she wasn't utterly crushed, that she could treat him with the same offhand friendliness with which he'd treated her tonight.

Turning over in bed, she clutched both edges of the pillow. Go to sleep. If she didn't get to sleep soon, she, too, might find herself defeated by Mr. Bokarski's Slavic-flavored dictation tomorrow.

Two blocks away, in her rent-controlled basement apartment on Eighty-sixth Street, May Cosgrove sat with her radio turned to a Connecticut radio station, one which from ten until midnight played light classics and the pleasant sort of songs Bing Crosby used to sing.

To Mrs. Cosgrove, hers wasn't a basement apartment, but a garden apartment. And indeed there was a big square of cement beyond the back door, with an eighteen-inch strip of earth on three sides separating it from a tall fence of wooden palings. In the almost thirty years she'd lived there, Mrs. Cosgrove had been unable to grow anything out there in the rubbly earth except a few geraniums and, in one corner, a privet bush. But it was nice to see the privet bush leaf out each spring. In fact, she was so pleased with her apartment, and felt so guilty about paying so little for it, that she'd granted the landlord several voluntary rent increases, even though he never kept his promise to do something about those noisy steampipes which ran across the ceiling.

Sitting there in her small rocker, once her aunt's, Mrs. Cosgrove reflected that it was indeed unfortunate that the little Wentworth girl had come back. Not that she wasn't a thoroughly nice child, a Gemini, like Mrs. Cosgrove herself, and with a lovely aureole. But the forces of evil were strong, as Mrs. Cosgrove knew and even a well-bred girl with a lovely aureole could become an unwitting instrument in their hands.

May Cosgrove had seen many aureoles, but never one as splendidly brilliant as David Bryant's. When he first came to the hill with his Great Dane one night three years before, she'd had to suppress a gasp of astonishment at sight of the brilliant circle of blue-white radiance above his head. And a second or so later, in tones of unmistakable clarity, an inner voice had told her that this man was the new—

Her thoughts hesitated. "Messiah" was the actual word that had come to her that night. But the influence of her Episcopalian upbringing was still too strong to allow her to feel comfortable with that word. Guru, on the other hand, was too weak. There were many gurus. "Teacher" seemed the best choice. David Bryant was to be the Great New Teacher who'd lead the world away from war and hatred and every other sort of wickedness.

Turning, she looked at the small table where, in front of David's framed picture, a small candle burned. She'd scissored the picture out of a newspaper the morning after his music had won the TV award. Often in the evenings she burned a candle before it.

During both of his visits here, she'd had the picture hidden away, of course. (What wonderful chats those had been! How his face had shone with fascinated interest as he sat there, listening to her and drinking tea from her grandmother's spode cup.) On both occasions she'd been tempted to tell him of the exalted role he was to play, but of course she hadn't. At the ordained moment, he himself would realize his high destiny. And then certain unfortunate aspects of his apparent nature—his taste for stimulants, for instance, and his occasional indulgence in frivolous or even ribald remarks—would drop from him, like an outworn garment.

In the meantime, perhaps she was the only person who knew of his future role, and of the powerful and dangerous forces arrayed against him. Certainly she was the only one of that group on the hill who realized the true significance of the events of that awful night. When David staggered back to the group, leaning on Henry Maize's shoulder, and told them, almost sobbing, that without meaning to he had taken a human life, she had realized instantly that the forces of darkness had moved to destroy him. They'd worked through a human being, of course, a thoroughly evil one, from the few stumbling words David had said about him. *He* was the real criminal.

Through the soft radio music, she spoke the man's loathsome name aloud. "Slide Thompson," she said. Probably Slide was only a nickname. Little as she knew about jazz musicians, she imagined they must give each other nicknames, the way athletes did.

Anyway, she was proud that she'd been the one most helpful to David that night. It was to her that he'd handed what, she supposed, the newspapers would call "the murder weapon." She'd brought it home in her purse. Later that night, working in the pitch blackness where two sides of the high paling fence met, she'd dug up her privet bush, dropped that ugly thing into the hole, and replanted the bush. It had taken her until two in the morning, but she'd done it. She hoped the bush would live. No plant should have its roots disturbed during the winter months, of course, but privet was so hardy that it might recover.

Her black-and-tan, Sistie, got up from her semicircular dog bed of red corduroy and ambled across the room to have her ears scratched. May Cosgrove loved Sistie, but deplored her arrogance. "Why," she asked, smoothing the dog's head, "do you have to be such a bully? Terrorizing that poor Bozo tonight!"

The Wentworth girl. Surely David had been prudent enough to ensure that she would stay away from the hill after this. Surely he realized how dangerous she could become. Unlike May Cosgrove herself, the child wouldn't think in terms of the higher morality. She'd go to the police.

Yes, surely Karen wouldn't come back to the hill tomorrow night.

If she did, something would have to be done about it.

5

The next afternoon, emerging into the early dark from the Sixty-third Street building that housed Bokarski Films, Karen decided to walk home rather than fight her way onto a subway car or bus. True, the temperature hovered around freezing, and sooty snow, with almost every imaginable sort of trash embedded in it, still lay heaped in the gutters. But after a day spent sorting out the confusion left by a series of "office temporaries," she felt keyed-up as well as tired. A walk would do her good.

Should she go up Third Avenue, or Second? Second, she decided, for no reason clear to her at the moment.

She'd walked twelve blocks north, through the sidewalk crowd of hurrying, tired-faced people, before she realized her reason for taking that route home. It concerned David, of course. Unconsciously she'd recalled that his sister had her photographic studio on Second Avenue, with living quarters above. Her intelligence had told her she must forget David as soon as possible, but something willful, perhaps even hopeful, within her had sought out this reminder of him.

The studio was still open, spilling light from the glass upper half of its door and from its broad display window. Pausing, Karen looked in at the framed photographs arranged against a dark green velvet curtain. Photographs of brides, and children, and family groups, and one of a gray-haired couple standing beside a wedding cake with the words "Golden Anniversary" written in icing on its lower tier. Did Consuelo, hanging over a darkroom tray as such photographs took shape in the developing fluid, ever feel a stab of bleak frustration? Or was she as self-sufficient as she seemed to be?

The display window light went out. Before Karen could turn away, the shop door opened and Consuelo emerged, a key in her hand. She halted, stared at Karen with chocolate-brown eyes, and then said, "Oh! Hello."

Karen smiled nervously. David's sister, with her level stare, her clipped speech, had always made her a little nervous. "I was admiring your photographs. I mean, I decided to walk home—"

Consuelo's brief nod might have meant almost anything, or nothing. She turned toward a doorway which led to a flight of stairs. "Well, me for a liedown before I start my supper."

"I'd better go home, too. See you in the park."

Consuelo turned back. "Tonight?"

"Why, of course."

Consuelo said after a moment, "I doubt that David will be there. Probably he's already walked Britt. He's having dinner with his girl and her parents at their house in Beekman Place."

Karen's smile felt rigid. "Oh?"

"I'm sure they'll marry soon. She's a beautiful girl, and they have so much in common. She's a concert pianist."

"She sounds marvelous." Fighting pain, Karen turned and walked away.

A concert pianist. A girl who must be at least somewhat well known. Odd that Consuelo hadn't mentioned her name. In fact, Consuelo's whole manner had seemed odd, somehow forced and false, almost as if the beautiful and rich concert pianist had been a hurried invention.

But why should Consuelo lie? True, Karen had been aware that David's sister hadn't been enthusiastic about her, but at least she'd tolerated her. It seemed unlikely that Consuelo would make up such a story just to cause additional pain. Besides, an interest in a new girl was the most logical explanation for David's behavior.

You weren't going to brood about it, she reminded herself. Just as she'd planned, she'd go to the hill for a few more nights. If David was about to marry, then it was even more important to show him she had no hard feelings, and the others that she had no intention of drooping like a blighted flower.

She moved up Second Avenue, past restaurants and grocery stores and antique shops, past that dating bar where she'd spent such an unrewarding evening. She'd just turned north on Eighty-fourth Street when she saw Evelyn Krim moving toward her, pulled at what must have been an uncomfortably fast pace by her small, detestable dog, Hawthorne.

An NYU sophomore with an overweight body and a bad skin, Evelyn was made doubly unfortunate by her ownership of Hawthorne. "The poor girl's living in a fool's paradise," David had once said of Evelyn. "That thing she has on a leash is not a dog. It's a rat." And indeed, despite Evelyn's insistence that Hawthorne was half dachshund and half terrier, there was something ratlike about his low-slung, rough-coated body, glittering small eyes, and vile disposition. Last fall and winter, Evelyn had tried to make herself and her pet a part of the group on the hill. But after several evenings, during which Hawthorne had launched himself hysterically at all the other dogs, including David's Great Dane, and nipped Paul Winship's ankle twice, Evelyn announced that Hawthorne was to undergo psychotherapy and wouldn't be brought to the hill again until his "emotional difficulties" had been straightened out.

Karen said, "Hello, Evelyn."

Hawthorne's owner hauled him to a stop. "Hi! So you're back." A sensitive girl, she hesitated. "Does that mean your father—?"

"He's going to be fine."

"Oh, I'm so glad. You still got your dog, Karen?"

"Yes. He flew down to Raleigh and back with me."

"Have you taken him up to the hill?"

"Yes." Then, swiftly: "How's Hawthorne?"

Evelyn's round face brightened. "Much better. That dog psychotherapist said Hawthorne was one of his most successful cases."

Karen look down at the dog, who responded with a sneer that displayed alarmingly long fangs. "Of course," Evelyn said hastily, "if anyone reaches down to pet him— But he doesn't bite people's ankles now, and he doesn't attack other dogs. Just snarls."

"Have you tried him on the hill since his treatments?"

Evelyn appeared suddenly subdued. "Yes. Just before I went home for Christmas vacation I took him up there, and everyone said he behaved quite well. But then I went home to Detroit, and I had flu, and I didn't get back until two weeks after college reopened, and anyway, when I got Hawthorne out of his boarding kennel and took him up to the hill—well, everybody acted as if he had rabies and I had bubonic plague." She paused, and then burst out, "Honestly, Karen, you'd have thought they'd heard something awful about me, so awful they didn't want me anywhere near. I went home and cried, and I never took Hawthorne to the hill again."

Looking into the other girl's disconsolate face, Karen felt an odd stilling of all her senses. In her distress over David, she'd almost forgotten the cool behavior of the others toward her. But if they'd treated Evelyn the same way . . .

She asked, "When did you get back from Detroit?"

"The fifteenth of January. Why?"

Then between December eighteenth, say, and the middle

of January, perhaps some trouble had descended upon those seven people accustomed to meeting each night. Some trouble that had drawn them into a tight little circle from which Karen herself and Evelyn and everyone else must be excluded.

"Why?" Evelyn repeated. "Why did you ask when I got back?"

Karen hesitated. She had no right to pass on her suspicion—a highly improbable one, if you thought about it. After all, the Kinsings and David and the rest were all respectable middle-class New Yorkers. What sort of shameful or dangerous secret could seven such people share?

She said, "Oh, I just wondered." Then: "Maybe you just imagined the people on the hill were unfriendly."

"I did not! And I'll have nothing more to do with them. I don't mean you, Karen. In fact, some night when my homework isn't too heavy, would it be okay if I call you? Maybe we could go to the movies."

"I'd like that. Well," Karen said, "I'd better get home."

An hour later, after she'd collected her dog from Mrs. Orford's apartment and fed him, she and Bozo moved west along Eighty-fourth Street. The temperature had dropped a few degrees during the past hour, and a chill wind blew down the concrete canyon between the apartment house walls, making her grateful for her dog-walking costume of fur hood, car coat, and felt-lined boots.

Ever since she'd turned away from Evelyn Krim, her puzzled and uneasy thoughts had kept circling around the group on the hill. Whatever the reason for their behavior, she'd finally decided, it was no concern of hers. As she'd planned, she'd greet them pleasantly but casually, and allow Bozo to play with the other dogs for a few minutes. Then, when she felt she'd proved she wasn't crushed by David's defection, she'd turn away.

Pausing at a traffic light at Madison, she saw Henry Maize and his cocker spaniel, on the opposite side of the avenue, turn up Eighty-fourth Street toward the park. In the past she might have hurried to catch up with him, because she'd liked the quiet middle-aged widower. But on the previous night his manner had been as distant as the others'. She waited a few seconds after the light turned, and then crossed the avenue.

At the foot of the hill, she saw that during the day children must have been using it as a slide for their sleds and aluminum "flying saucers." They'd packed the snow hard, and now, with the drop in temperature, a broad sheet of ice had formed, gleaming dully in the light from the standard lamp. With Bozo pulling at the leash, she climbed through the unimpacted snow close to the museum wall, and then circled around to the group standing on the hill's crest. With mingled relief and wry disappointment, she saw that David wasn't among them. Did the concert pianist really exist, then? Or had David merely taken Britt across the road? Often in the past, leaving the group for fifteen minutes or so, he'd taken the Great Dane to the broad meadow about two hundred yards deeper in the park, so that she could run freely.

Karen said, approaching the group, "Hi, everybody."

"Good evening," Mrs. Cosgrove answered, and George Kinsing said, in a constrained voice, "Hello, Karen."

For a few seconds there was silence. Then Doris Kinsing, her face framed in a mink-trimmed woolen hood, turned to Karen and said clearly, "We were just talking about you."

Karen's nerves tightened. Doris's tone and her faint smile clearly implied that the talk hadn't been favorable. Trying to keep her voice light, Karen said, "You were?"

"We were wondering why you come clear up here, when the park over on the East River is so much closer to you."

Still trying to sound pleasant, Karen said, "It's only about a block closer. Besides, Bozo doesn't like Carl Schurz Park. Too much concrete." The truth was that she'd walked the extra block that first night because she loved the dramatic contrast between Central Park's hills and ponds and woodland and the tall buildings hemming it in. After that first night, of course, there'd been the additional and more compelling reason of David.

Doris said, with insulting persistence, "Well, it does seem odd that a girl should go out of her way night after night to come here." Where she isn't wanted, her tone clearly added.

No one said anything. Karen had a sense that each of them, even gentle-faced May Cosgrove, was waiting for the insult to take effect.

Quite suddenly, and for no reason she could define, she was afraid of them. Even though no one had moved, she felt as if they'd formed a menacing circle around her. . . .

Then, through that fear, her anger flared. "What seems odd," she said in a high, clear voice, "is that you should discuss my coming here. May I remind you that this is a public park? I'll come to any part of it, including this hill, just as often as I choose."

She turned away, pulling at Bozo's leash. From the corner of her eye, she caught a glimpse of David and his Great Dane across the automobile road that curved through the park, waiting for a break in the stream of traffic. She didn't pause. Pulling the reluctant Bozo after her, she skirted the top of that icy strip at the center of the slope, and then hurried down the hill toward Fifth Avenue.

For perhaps a minute after she left, no one spoke or moved. Then Henry Maize bent toward the black cocker spaniel which, twelve years before when it was a puppy, he'd brought home to his wife as a birthday gift. Even though he'd unleashed the dog, she stood close beside him, her dull black fur pressed against his leg. He snapped on her leash. "Come on, Fluff. Let us two old crocks go home."

Five minutes later, he and the dog rose in a self-service elevator to the fourth floor of an apartment building on Eighty-fifth Street. Leaving his galoshes at the door, he turned the key in the lock and entered his too silent, too orderly apartment. He unleashed Fluff and walked into the bedroom, intending to take off his plaid mackinaw. Instead he sank down on the edge of one of the twin beds and stared at the other one.

After Myra's death, he'd given her clothes to the Salvation Army. Why hadn't he given her bed away, too? Why, after ten years, was he still unable to bear the thought of some stranger lying in her bed?

He said aloud, "Myra, you shouldn't have left me. If you'd lived, I wouldn't be in this mess of Bryant's."

If Myra had lived, David Bryant wouldn't have asked for a lift up to Massachusetts that summer three years ago. He wouldn't have asked, because Henry and Myra themselves wouldn't have been going up there. During their first and only stay at their son's new home, their daughter-in-law Maureen, a high-strung, compulsively neat young woman, had been unable to hide her distress over her disrupted household, with the twin boys sleeping on makeshift beds on the sunporch so that their grandparents could have a bedroom, and their grandfather's diet requiring specially prepared foods.

On their way home, Henry and Myra had decided that in the future they'd wait for the young people to visit them in New York. But in the lonely years after his wife's death, he found himself unable to decline those annual invitations to "spend the first week of your vacation with us," even though he knew how reluctantly those invitations were issued.

And so, standing on the Central Park hill that hot August evening three years ago, with reflected sunset light blazing down from Fifth Avenue windows, he'd mentioned that he was driving up to Massachusetts after work the next day.

David Bryant asked, "Your son lives near Graham Falls, doesn't he?"

"Twenty miles north of there."

"I'm invited to Graham Falls for the weekend. My car's laid up, so I planned to take the train. But how about my

43

hitching a ride with you?"

Even though Henry, without knowing why, had never liked David much, he felt he couldn't refuse him a ride. Besides, David's company might distract him from the mingled anticipation and dread with which he always approached his son's house.

"Glad to have you," Henry said. "Suppose we meet at my place at six."

"Great. I'll buy us dinner on the way."

Apparently David had been in his most agreeable mood the next evening. As they drove north out of the city and then east toward the Connecticut line, he turned the conversation to fishing, a topic dear to Henry's heart. By the time they stopped at a restaurant near Torrington, Henry was thoroughly enjoying himself. He accepted two martinis and, after a moment's hesitation, agreed with David's suggestion that they have wine with the dinner. A hearty meal would counter the effects of the alcohol.

When they emerged into the darkness to resume their journey, Henry felt entirely sober. Still perhaps his reaction time had been affected. Perhaps without the drinks he'd have slowed when he saw the hitchhiker—here on the parkway, where hitchhikers were forbidden—standing a foot or so inside the road's edge, arm raised and thumb cocked, his face shadowed by the sort of wide-brimmed straw hat Puerto Rican migratory workers often wear.

But he hadn't slowed. There'd been a sickening impact. As if in a dream, he'd seen the thin body, in white trousers and a red shirt angle through the air away from the headlights' path, and strike against the concrete wall of an underpass.

Had he stopped then, even momentarily? Henry couldn't remember, and he never asked David afterward. All he knew was that sometime later he saw an *Emergency Parking* sign loom up ahead. At the same moment, that dreamlike sense dissolved, letting cold horror flood in upon him. Turning off the highway onto the deserted strip of asphalt, he stopped and switched off the headlights.

He heard his own voice. "What shall I do?"

"That's up to you, isn't it?"

"But I don't know what to do."

"As I said, it's your decision. But you realize it's almost certain the man is dead, don't you? Going back wouldn't change that."

Dead. Yes, he must be. First the impact of the car, then the concrete wall. Looking into the rear-view mirror, Henry watched a car pass along the highway. A few seconds later three more passed, in a group, and then, after an interval, four more cars bunched together. Since traffic was moving along the highway at normal speeds and in normal groupings, it seemed unlikely that any of those drivers had seen the body. Perhaps it had fallen down among the bushes against the underpass wall. If so, it might remain undiscovered until morning. On the other hand, perhaps right at this moment the lights of some slow-moving patrol car were picking out a white trouser leg, the sleeve of a bright red shirt.

If he went back now, with liquor on his breath, and found the police there, he'd probably get at least a year, perhaps more. And he'd lose his job and his pension rights. What insurance company could afford to have on its payroll a claims adjustor who, under the influence of alcohol, had committed vehicular homicide?

And there was his son's wife. She'd have every excuse now to keep him away from his grandsons and the little granddaughter Myra had never seen, but whose grave, quiet ways reminded him so much of his wife. It would be cruel to the children, he could imagine Maureen saying, to have their friends teasing them about having a convict for a grandfather.

He switched on the headlights. Getting out, he went to the front of the car. Just as he'd thought, the right side of the front end was damaged. He couldn't see any blood, but nevertheless he took out his pocket handkerchief and wiped the crumpled metal. With luck, he could get safely to Graham Falls, only fifteen miles away. After all, you saw many damaged cars moving along the parkways. From there he'd take a little-used country road to his son's house.

After forty minutes driven in complete silence, he stopped midway of Graham Falls' darkened Main Street. "Here all right?"

"Yes." David got out and then, bending, looked back into the car. For the first time, Henry emerged sufficiently from his guilty wretchedness to wonder at the younger man's motives. Why hadn't David urged him to turn back? Out of friendship? But despite those almost nightly meetings, they were only acquaintances. Compassion? Henry didn't think so. Self-interest? Probably. At twenty-seven, David was becoming fairly well known in musical circles. He'd just as soon not have his name connected with a hit-and-run death.

Henry said in a voice heavy with self-loathing, "What if I'm caught?"

David's voice was calm. "I'll stay in the clear. I'll say I fell asleep after we left the restaurant. The martinis, you know, and the wine. I felt an impact and woke up, but you said you'd just hit a chuckhole in the road. I went back to sleep and stayed asleep until you woke me up to let me off here. Well, good night, Henry."

He crossed the street and moved away up the sidewalk. Henry drove on.

The driveway to his son's house, a red brick Georgian surrounded by an iron picket fence, was flanked by two stone pillars. As he'd planned to, Henry turned his car off the road and aimed its right headlight at one of the pillars. There was the grind of metal against stone, and a tinkle of glass. He saw the porch light go on, and, as he backed away, the figures of his son and daughter-in-law hurrying down the steps. They'd suspect him of drunkenness, of

46

course. And he'd have to have the pillar repaired at his own expense. Still, that was a small price to pay—very small.

He'd learned, of course, that the price was much higher than that. Part of the payment was the stomach-knotting dread with which, for days, he'd tuned in news broadcasts and opened newspapers. The body, he knew, couldn't have remained undiscovered for more than eight hours. But apparently the death of a migrant, one who probably hadn't been able to read the English-language signs which forbade hitchhiking, hadn't been considered news.

He shrank from the thought of seeing David again. But when he returned to New York, it seemed to him wrong to deprive Fluff of her canine friends. Besides, the conviviality of those brief nightly gatherings had assumed importance in his lonely, routine life. And so, the night after he retrieved Fluff from her boarding kennel, he took her up to the hill. David's pleasant but casual manner toward him seemed no different than before that terrible moment on the parkway. As the months passed, Henry came to feel that no more penalties would be exacted from him—except, of course, those exacted by his own knowledge of his carelessness and cowardice.

But he'd learned there was still another penalty that night three weeks ago when, through a curtain of snowflakes, he'd seen one of those two dark figures crumple to the ground. The price for having evaded the penalty for one violent death, he'd realized within the next few minutes, was to keep silent about another.

Again he stared at the other bed, with its smooth counterpane of green corduroy. If Myra had been with him that night on the parkway, she wouldn't have allowed him to drive on. In Myra's gentle character, there'd been a vein of moral iron.

Karen Wentworth had impressed him as being like that. Therefore he'd hated seeing her fall for David Bryant. Well, he was sorry to see her hurt now, and yet the one good thing about the whole wretched business was that it had forced David Bryant to thrust her out of his life. If she did but know it, she was lucky.

Getting heavily to his feet, he took off his old mackinaw and hung it in the closet.

6

As it turned out, Karen didn't take her dog to any part of the park the next night, because when she came home from the office, she found that Bozo had disappeared.

As usual, she'd rung the bell of her landlady's apartment. Opening the door, Mrs. Orford said, "Hello, dear." Then, glancing toward the floor, "So you didn't pick up Bozo?"

"Pick him up! What do you mean? Isn't he here?"

Astonishment crossed the older woman's face. "Why, no, dear. About three o'clock this Chinese girl showed up. Or maybe Japanese. Anyway, one of those dog walkers. I've seen her in the neighborhood with as many as six dogs at a time. She said that she was from the Bill Bailey Kennels, and that you'd asked to have your dog picked up. I was surprised, but I figured you wanted to have Bozo given a flea bath or something."

"I didn't!" With growing alarm, she started to turn away, and then paused. "Bill Bailey's, you said?"

"Yes. It's on Eighty-second, almost on the corner of Fifth Avenue."

"I know." She headed for the door.

Five minutes later, a little winded from the swift pace which had brought her there, she leaned against an areaway railing and saw, in a basement office, a brown-haired young man seated at a desk beneath a green-shaded droplight.

Scowling, he stared down at an open ledger.

Karen ran down the steps, punched a doorbell. After a moment the door opened. "Yes?" He was twenty-eight or so, a tall man with rugged features. Evidently he scowled a lot, because even now, when he was smiling, there were horizontal grooves across his forehead.

She asked, not returning the smile, "Are you Mr. Bailey?"

"That's right."

"I've come for my dog!"

Her tone brought mild astonishment to his face. "Sure," he said, and opened the door wide. As she moved past him into the office, he asked, "Which dog is yours?"

"He's a collie—well, part collie." The woman at the ASPCA had been sure he was also part hound, perhaps bloodhound. "One of your dog walkers picked him up today and—"

"I was at our Brooklyn branch all day. But if you ordered him picked up, he must be back in the kennel."

"I didn't order it! One of your dog walkers just came and took him from my landlady. She was a Chinese girl."

"That's impossible. Unless she was requested to, Mary Ching would never have—"

"I tell you she did! And I want my dog."

"All right," he said hastily. "Let's look."

He opened a door in the far wall, stood aside, and let her precede him into a long, cement-floored room lined with cages. At the other end of the room, in a straight chair tilted against the wall, a youth of about seventeen sat reading a comic book.

Their entrance set off a chorus of barks and whines. "Quiet!" Bill Bailey said. Except for one defiant yip, the dogs fell silent.

Followed by the kennel owner, Karen moved swiftly down the aisle between the cages. A blond Afghan. A red setter. Two German shepherds. Two standard and one miniature poodle. But no long-haired dog with a crumpled ear and a wide grin.

She whirled around. "He isn't here! He's been stolen! That dog walker of yours—"

"Now wait a minute!" He was scowling now. "I don't employ thieves. Besides, who'd steal a dog like that?"

She said with mounting anxiety and anger, "What do you mean, a dog like that? What are you? Some kind of racist?"

"Racist!"

"Yes!" Dimly she realized that the youth with the comic book was staring at her. "Let me tell you, my dog is just as good as any of these, and perhaps in some ways better. Why, he doesn't even like to use the gutter. He waits until he gets up to the bushes in the park—"

"Now just calm down! I'm not interested in your dog's personal habits, fascinating as they may be. All I meant was that crossbreeds aren't stolen for resale to pet shops. As for the creeps that steal dogs and sell them to laboratories, they don't bother to get jobs as dog walkers. They just pick up strays, or take dogs left in front of supermarkets. Now come on. I'll phone Mary Ching."

In his office a moment later, Karen heard him say into the phone, "Mary? Did you pick up a crossbreed today from—?" He looked inquiringly at Karen. She gave him the address, and he relayed it into the phone. "You did? Where is the dog now?"

After a moment he hung up. "She says a telegram came," he muttered, and reached for a spindle on his desk. Impaled upon it were a number of papers, including a yellow rectangular one. He read the wire, stood up, and, without comment, handed it to Karen.

Addressed to Bill Bailey Kennels, the telegram said: "Please pick up my dog from the manager at 317 East Eighty-fourth Street and take it to Randalls Pet Shop. I'll pick it up there later."

The wire was signed "Karen Wentworth."

"Did you send that?"

Still staring at the telegram, she shook her head.

"Some sort of practical joke, huh? Fine friends you've got."

Then he saw she'd turned so pale that the dusting of freckles across her nose seemed to stand out. "Give me that." Taking the telegram from her hand, he folded it and placed it in his shirt pocket. He moved toward his duffel coat, hanging from a coat tree in one corner. "The pet shop's only a few blocks south on Madison." He put on the coat, opened the door to the kennels, and called, "Joe! Answer the phone if it rings, will you?"

Out on the sidewalk Karen asked in a thin voice, "What if he's not there?"

"He'll be there. That's a reliable shop." Then, after they'd turned onto Madison Avenue: "Any idea who pulled this stunt?"

"Not exactly." But she was sure one of them had done it. Which one? David? Oh, surely not. Whoever it had been, though, the message was clear. "Stay away from us." Perhaps, too, there was a footnote which read, "If you don't, something really bad will happen to your dog, or to you."

Beneath her anxiety, a hot rage stirred. Whoever had done this wouldn't be allowed to go unchallenged.

She said, "Didn't you—I mean, whoever you left in charge today, didn't they think it was odd, getting a telegram instead of a phone call?"

"Odd? Sure. But plenty of crazy things happen in this business. A woman yesterday bawled the devil out of me because I wouldn't send someone to walk her pet skunk. Besides, with phone service the way it is, a lot of people have been driven to sending telegrams."

They'd reached the pet shop. In one window, three boxer puppies drank from a water dish, and in the other two Siamese kittens lay asleep. Bill Bailey opened the door.

The moment Karen entered, hysterical barking issued from behind the bars of a low steel cage at the far end of the long room. A smiling, eyeglassed woman said, "I gather that's your dog," and walked over to unfasten the cage. Crouching, Karen braced herself to receive Bozo's joyous rush.

She was still rubbing his coat and turning her head to avoid the dog's moist tongue when the eyeglassed woman said, "Here's his leash. That'll be six dollars, please."

Feeling a little dazed with relief, Karen stood up. "Six dollars?"

"That's the charge for twenty-four hours, or any fraction thereof."

Wincing inwardly, Karen opened her red shoulder bag. There went that paisley scarf she'd planned to buy this week. But no matter. She had her dog back.

Bill Bailey said, "Send me the bill, Mrs. Randall."

Karen protested, "Oh, you mustn't."

"Send me the bill," he repeated. He grasped Karen's arm. "Come on. Let's go."

They retraced their steps along Madison Avenue. Karen said, "You didn't have to do that. None of this was your fault."

"It won't be six dollars. She'll give me a professional discount, same as I would her. Now what you need after all this is a good dinner. How about that new French restaurant on Eighty-sixth Street?"

"I told you it was all right. You don't have to feel—"

He stopped short, brow furrows deepening with exasperation. "Damn it all! Of course I don't have to. I want to. And you know why? It's because you're so damned ugly. Nothing turns me on like looking across a restaurant table at an ugly girl."

She laughed then. "I'd like going to dinner very much."

"Good." As they walked on, he said, "I'll have to change clothes. Why don't you wait in the office for me? My apartment's right upstairs."

"All right. Then could we stop by my place so that I

can change? It won't take me more than a few minutes."

"I may not know much about women, but I do know it'll take you at least half an hour. While you're dressing, I'll take your dog over to the bushes in Carl Schurz Park."

Later that evening, as they sat over onion soup in the Eighty-sixth Street restaurant, Karen asked, "Is your name really Bill Bailey?"

He nodded. "William Trevor Bailey, known since early childhood as Bill." His tone became apprehensive. "You're not going to hand me some witticism about why don't I go home, are you?"

"I wouldn't dream of it. How did you get into the dog business?"

"Inherited it from my father, who was also Bill Bailey. The Manhattan place, anyway. I started the Brooklyn kennel six months ago."

"Do you like this sort of business?"

"Sure. It's crazy, in both senses of the word." He told her, then, about some of the more far-out members of his clientele. There was the anxiety-prone violinist, a novice dog owner, who'd besought him to recommend "a competent dog obstetrician" for his pregnant Dalmatian. There was also a seldom-employed TV comic who dressed his female boxer in a red plastic coat emblazoned with his own name before sending her out with a dog walker.

In return, Karen told him about some Bokarski Films misadventures, including a movie they'd made, at the behest of the Long Island Railroad, to persuade school children not to throw rocks at train windows. Soon after its release, Mr. Bokarski and the railroad found themselves in the lamentable position of the woman who warned her offspring not to stick beans up their noses. Children to whom it had never occurred to break train windows began swarming down to the tracks, pockets loaded with stones.

It wasn't until they were having coffee that Bill said, "When I went up to my place to dress, I called Western

54

Union. According to their records, the wire was phoned in from a pay telephone. It was a Regent Four number, so that telephone must be in this neighborhood. I asked if it was a man or a woman who'd called. They said they had no record of that, and doubt that the day clerk who took the message would remember."

A pay phone in this neighborhood. Well, that didn't help. They all lived in this neighborhood.

Bill had been watching her closely. "You have some idea of who sent it, don't you?"

"More or less." Doris Kinsing might have done it, or Consuelo Bryant. After all, apparently she'd lied about David's having an "early dinner date" with a pianist, or anyone else. And Paul Winship might have done it. Listening to his stories about "the old biddies" or "blowzy babes" who bought ties for their menfolk at his counter, she'd long been aware that he felt an especial malice toward women.

But she had no right, at this point, to voice a suspicion of anyone to Bill. She had even less right to speak of the shadowy and chilling idea which had lingered, half formed, at the back of her mind ever since she'd looked up the hill Monday night and seen that once lively group, now so strangely quiet, standing near the crest of the hill.

"Yes, I feel that one of several people might have sent that wire. I'd rather not talk about it now, though." But tomorrow night she'd talk to *them* about it. She'd say plenty.

Bill asked slowly, "Karen, are you in any sort of trouble?"

"No. At least I don't think so."

"If you find that you are, will you come to me about it? Maybe I could help."

Until now, when she felt a kind of warmth spreading all through her, she hadn't known that David's apparent loss of interest had brought her more than pain and humiliation. It had made her feel lonely, too—even lonelier than she'd been her first week in New York.

She smiled at him. "Yes, I'll come to you if I need help."

7

The temperature dropped into the middle twenties the next day. Thus that evening, when Karen and Bozo climbed the hill, skirting that broad icy strip down the middle, their feet broke through a thickened snow crust at every step.

Purposely, she'd come to the hill about fifteen minutes later than in the old days, hoping to find the group intact—the late arrivers already there, and the early ones still lingering. As she drew close to the little knot of people, she saw with grim satisfaction that her timing had been perfect.

Without preamble she said in a cool, clear voice, "Which one of you kidnaped my dog?"

For a few seconds no one answered. Then Paul Winship said, "Doll, I'm afraid you've flipped your wig. Nobody kidnaped your dog. There he is, on the other end of that leash you're holding."

She glanced down. Bozo lay with paws in the air. May Cosgrove's Sistie, stump of a tail wagging, gave a few ritual growls as she sniffed at his throat.

"I know he's here now! But yesterday somebody had him picked up and taken to a pet shop. Somebody sent a wire, in my name." Anger thickened her voice. "Now which one of you did it?"

No one spoke. Her gaze swept the circle of faces. Every one of them looked troubled. Even David's face had lost its assurance, at least momentarily. That slight, malicious smile of Paul Winship's had died, and May Cosgrove's usually serene features appeared tense.

"All right!" she said vaguely but furiously. "There's only one thing I have to say. I don't know what you're up to. But don't any of you ever do anything to me again, or to my dog. Next time, I'll go straight to the police."

Pulling Bozo to his feet, she started down the hill.

With angry dismay, David stared after her for a second or two. Then he whistled Britt to him, and attached the Great Dane's heavy chain leash. Who'd sent that wire? Doris Kinsing? Consuelo? No, Doris was too stupid to think up such a stunt, and his sister too bright to carry it out. It must have been that batty May Cosgrove. Without even saying good night to the others, he set off after Karen.

He caught up with her before she reached Fifth Avenue. "Hey!" he said, touching her arm. "What's the rush?"

She stopped and looked up into his face. He was smiling, gray eyes crinkled at the corners. "No rush," she said coolly. "It was just that I'd said what I had to say."

"Karen, did someone really have your dog taken away? Oh, I believe you," he added hastily. "It's just that it seems such a senseless trick. Mean, too, of course." When she didn't answer, he said in a grave tone, "You don't think I did it, do you?"

"No," she answered after a moment, "but somebody did."

"Well, maybe over dinner we can figure out who, and why. What's the matter? Don't you want to have dinner with me? You used to like it, or seemed to."

"It's just that I didn't expect— I mean, you seemed so— strange last Monday night. And when we got to Lexington Avenue—" Her throat closed up with the remembered pain of looking after him as he walked away.

"Darling, can you forgive me for that? I realized later how odd my behavior must have seemed. But I'd felt it was better for us to postpone your welcome-back celebration. I

57

was in a rotten mood. I didn't want to tell you about it—it's so damned *dull*—but the income tax people had been bugging me about last year's return. I went down to the tax office today and got it straightened out. It was their mistake," he added in a tone of relish.

She looked up at him, undecided. Income tax hassles were not unfamiliar to her. Once her father had carried on a long correspondence with the tax people about a deduction for some stolen medical instruments. And last spring, when she first reported to work at Bokarski Films, she'd found a grim-faced Internal Revenue man in Mr. Bokarski's office, and Mr. Bokarski himself alternating between Slavic rage and Slavic despair.

Could it be that she'd misinterpreted David's behavior entirely? Then she remembered what his sister had said. "David, you don't have to be polite. Consuelo told me about your girl."

"My girl!" His astonishment was unmistakably genuine.

"That concert pianist. Consuelo said she's very lovely."

He groaned. "Sometimes I think my worst break happened before I was born. Why, oh, why, did my mother have to marry Consuelo's father? Now listen, Karen. The only lady concert pianist I know is what the French call of a certain age. And I doubt if she was ever lovely, except in Consuelo's imagination."

He glanced over his shoulder. "Here she comes now, with the Kinsings. Don't let them catch up with us."

Crossing Fifth Avenue, they moved at a brisk pace down Eighty-fourth Street. David said, "Suppose I nip over to my place when we get to Lexington. I'll pick you up in about forty minutes. Okay?"

He was behaving as if nothing had changed between them. Could it be that it hadn't, except in her own mind? Confused and hesitant, she said, "Well, all right."

"A new French place opened up on Eighty-sixth Street while you were away. Like to try it?"

Undoubtedly that was the place where she'd spent such a pleasant two hours with Bill Bailey the night before. Somehow she didn't want to go there with David. "If you don't mind—I mean, how about the Danube Inn?"

The Danube was a place that had always amused David. He called it "the very best low camp." She hadn't understood the term fully until they sat amid the Danube's frowzy grandeur—walls hung with frayed red velvet, an overweight "gypsy soprano" with fake eyelashes almost an inch long, a cymbalon and zither orchestra, and a strolling violinist who gazed soulfully into the eyes of lady patrons as he played "Golden Earrings."

"Great! The Danube it is. I haven't been there since you left town."

Except that there was a new gypsy soprano, the Danube hadn't changed. Over chicken paprika, and under the orchestra's frenzied rendition of "The Sabre Dance," David said, "Now tell me about Bozo being dognaped."

She told him about it, including her dinner with Bill Bailey. When she'd finished, he asked, after a moment, "Attractive guy?"

Not as attractive as David was. Nobody would think that. And yet— "He's very nice," she said. Then, quickly, "Do you think Consuelo sent that wire?"

"Why Consuelo?"

"Well, if she made that up about the pianist—"

"That's different. Kidnaping your dog was from Weirdsville, but Consuelo's story about my having another girl wasn't. From her point of view, telling a lie like that was a practical maneuver." His eyes looked directly into hers. "Whether my sister realizes it or not, she doesn't want to see me seriously interested in any girl. And she knows I feel very seriously about you."

It was a proposal, almost. What was wrong with her? Where was the leap of joy she should be feeling? Lowering her eyes, she took a sip from her water glass.

David said, "Not the right moment to talk about that, huh?"

"No, somehow it isn't."

"Karen, what's wrong? It's more than just that wire somebody sent, isn't it?"

"Well, yes. It's—all of you. The Kinsings, and Henry Maize, and—all of you. There's something withdrawn and secretive about you, almost as if—"

She broke off. Where had it come from, that warning that she'd been about to say too much? That sense of danger gathering itself in this gaudy room, like an animal tensing to spring?

"As if what?" He bit off the end of a breadstick and sat there chewing while a grin spread slowly over his face. "Like a conspiracy?" His smile widened. "I know. While you were away we formed a witches' covine, with May Cosgrove as our leader. Come Midwinters' Eve, we made a human sacrifice of some hapless soul. Then, after posting Paul Winship up by the road to watch for prowl cars, we all took off our clothes and danced in the snow. It was silly of the Romans to think that the ancient Britons painted themselves blue. They *were* blue, from all that nekkid dancing they did at druid ceremonials."

That sense of danger vanished under a flood of amused relief. He himself had conjured up that half-formed picture that had haunted her—the darkened parking lot, the upraised knife—and in doing so he'd made her realize how ridiculous it was.

She asked, laughing, "Did you beat drums, too?"

"We would have, except for the anti-noise ordinance."

"Oh, David!" Then, sobering: "But everybody did seem— unwelcoming. Evelyn Krim noticed it, too."

"Who?"

"You remember her. She's that girl who goes to NYU."

"Oh, yes. The one with that awful little dog. I remember now. She brought him up to the hill again one night last

60

January. Sure we all gave her the icy shoulder. If she can't bring herself to get rid of the beast, she at least ought not to inflict him on others."

That sounded reasonable. And yet Evelyn had said something else, something that eluded her memory. She had the feeling, though, that those forgotten words somehow contradicted the explanation he had just given.

"You're right though," he said, "about a certain chill having descended upon our once-happy little group. Doris Kinsing and Consuelo have created it. They've been feuding in a polite, bitchy way, although sometimes not so polite, and it puts a damper, so to speak."

"Feuding over you?"

"How do you mean?"

"You've said yourself that Consuelo is possessive. And it must be obvious to everyone, including poor George, that Doris thinks you're the most attractive thing since Paul Newman."

"Spare my blushes. Anyway, it isn't that. Their personalities clash, that's all." He leaned toward her, smiling. "Tell me. Did thoughts of a witches' covine cross your mind?"

"Of course not."

"Then what did? Come on. Level with Papa."

She said after a long moment, "Maybe you'll think I'm out of my skull. But before I went up to the hill Monday night, Mrs. Orford mentioned that—that a girl had been stabbed to death right there in the parking lot near the foot of the hill."

"And you thought—wow! The things that go on behind that lovely face, so open-looking, so quaintly and refreshingly calm in these days of blown minds and splintered psyches."

She felt color in her cheeks. "But everyone did seem so strange." Her tone sharpened. "And someone *did* have my dog taken away."

"Darling, I was just kidding." He reached across the table

61

and squeezed her hand briefly. "As for the girl, someone was killed in the parking lot. It happened the second or third of January, I think. Anyway, before I got back from Boston. The Boston Pops played a composition of mine for the first time, so I went up there."

"The one that got the award, *The Blue Planet Theme?*"

"Yes. By the time I got back, it wasn't in the papers anymore. You know how it is in this town. Unless a murder's pretty spectacular, or the people involved are important, it doesn't rate much newspaper space. But Consuelo and the others talked about it, since it had happened so close to the hill. And within about a week, as I recall, the man who'd done it was caught. He was either her husband or lover, I forget which. Anyway, he confessed."

Every word he'd said about the girl could be checked on easily. Feeling relief flood through her, she thought, "Why, I must have really suspected—"

Aloud she said, "Poor girl. But at least I'm glad they caught the man." She paused and then said with a smile, "I just recalled something I've been trying to remember. Evelyn also said that after her dog had been in the hands of some sort of trainer—a dog psychotherapist, I think she called him—she brought him up to the hill about a week before Christmas. You were all very nice to her, she said, and complimented her on how well Hawthorne behaved. But the next time she came up there, about the middle of January, all of you snubbed her. It really got me going."

"I don't remember her bringing her dog up there before Christmas, but maybe she did. Perhaps I wasn't on the hill that night. Anyway, you shouldn't pay any attention to her. She's neurotic where that dog is concerned. If you ask me, she's the one who needs a psychotherapist."

The waiter handed them menus. Karen said, studying the dessert list, "Well, it did bother me. I even thought of going down to the *New York Times* and looking through those microfilmed back copies for stories about that poor girl, or about anything else that happened in that part of the park around the holidays or a week or so after."

"Well, if you do look through that microfilm thing, take a magnifying glass with you. Otherwise you'll need dark specs and a tin cup afterwards. Those machines are hell on the eyes. How about Blueberry Torte à la Danube for dessert?"

"It's loaded with whipped cream."

"No matter. We can walk it off. Let's go down Second Avenue and look at all the wonderful junk in those antique shop windows. Whenever we feel tired or too cold, we'll stop in a pub."

It was past midnight when, at the corner of Second Avenue and Forty-ninth Street, Karen called a halt. They'd window-shopped for thirty blocks, stopping in three different bars for glasses of beer. With their Celtic names— Leary's, T. L. Muldoon's, Tim Flaherty's—each establishment had suggested a New York of many years ago, when transplanted Irishmen, leaving their wives at home in cold-water flats, had stood on sawdust-covered floors night after night, elbows propped on massive bars. Some of the places still affected sawdust, but the Irish clientele had been replaced by chic young eastside singles of both sexes.

Karen said, "It's been great fun, but I'd better go home now. Tomorrow's a working day."

"Okay, I'll get a cab." He turned toward the curb and then paused, an appalled look on his face. "Wait. I'd better check."

Taking out a black calfskin wallet, he looked inside it. "Just as I thought. One lousy dollar left. Well, maybe I've got enough change—" He plunged a hand into a trouser pocket and brought out coins. "Let's see. Two dimes, three pennies—"

"Oh, David! I've got enough money for a cab."

"Never! You haven't suspected it, but beneath this urbane exterior beats the heart of an unreconstructed male suprem-acist. I have subway tokens, and that's the way we'll get home. Or wait. I've got money at my place. You can wait in the cab while I go upstairs—"

"Oh, for heaven's sake. The subway will be fine. You know I even like it, except at rush hours."

Walking to the subway stop on Lexington, they descended cement steps. The man in the change booth, reading *The Daily News,* didn't even look up as they passed his glass-fronted cage. David dropped a token in the subway stile for Karen, and then another for himself.

At this late hour of a weekday night, the long subway platform lay deserted under the dim yellow lights. The air seemed colder and damper down here, with draughts eddying from the downtown platform across the tracks, and from the dark-mouthed tunnels. David gave a shiver. "Want to walk?"

They walked to the northern end of the long platform, turned, and walked back past the turnstiles, reading the ads and the graffiti on the wall as they went. (Someone, perhaps still in mourning for the mini skirt, had written on the white space of a department store ad: "Ladies! Why have you let Fashion enslave you?") At the far end of the platform they stopped, shivering, and now and then stamping their feet.

David asked suddenly, "You want some peanuts from the vending machine? Some of those nice, stale peanuts?"

"No, thanks. Besides, I think our train is coming." From somewhere deep in the tunnel she heard the screech of wheels against steel rails. Stirred by air, the train pushed ahead of it, a sheet of newspaper lying directly below her on the track fluttered into the air for a moment and then fell back, like a wounded bird.

David said, "Well, I want some. It will only take a second."

Aware that he'd walked away, she went on staring at the tunnel mouth. She was still enough of a newcomer to New York to find the subway intriguing. She liked to catch the first glimpse of a train's headlights as it approached a station. When alone on a train, she often stood on the front platform beside the motorman's steel-enclosed cab, enjoying the sense of increased speed and the sweep of the headlight along a curving tunnel wall.

She leaned forward a little over the platform's edge. The train must still be at least half a mile away, because she couldn't see its lights. But the cold wind pushed ahead of it had grown stronger. She could feel it lifting the hair from her forehead.

A split second later her body, pushed off balance by something or someone behind her, was slanting out over the platform's edge. Frantically, her hands clawed the air for support.

She was falling. Even though the tracks were only about five feet below the platform's edge, she seemed to go on falling for a long time, long enough for her to realize in every blood vessel, every inch of fragile flesh and crushable bone, what that approaching multi-tonned train was going to do to her.

The steel rails seemed to rise up to meet her, one striking her across the legs just below the knee, the other across her bent forearms. For an interval—timeless to her, but perhaps only a second or two—she lay stunned. Then the will to live, surging through her, brought her to her hands and knees. She rose, stumbled toward the platform, that platform with its outward jutting edge which she could never pull herself over in time to escape the steel monster. Its lights bathed her now, and the agonized screech of its brakes filled her ears.

Faces looking down at her. David's deathly white one, and another man's. Hands reaching down to her own frantically upstretched ones, and drawing her upward. Although she felt no pain, she was aware of her knee scraping over the steel band at the platform's edge.

She stood swaying, on the platform now, with David grasping one of her arms, and the strange man the other. Still a third man had joined them. As she looked at him his face, beneath a green felt hat, seemed to waver and change shape, as if seen through water.

Behind her the train screamed to a halt. As it did so, a black mist closed in around her.

She seemed to be lying on something hard. Eyes still closed—somehow she didn't want to open them—she heard David's voice. "— Bryant," he said. He gave his address. "You've got to believe me! I slipped on something and stumbled against her. Grease, maybe, or an orange peel. This filthy, filthy city! Anyway, I slipped. *You* fellows must have seen it. You must have been coming onto the platform just then."

A strange voice, a man's, said, "Maybe you did. It looked like you sort of fell against her." And then another man said, "You can't prove it by me. Anything more than twenty feet away, I'm blind as a bat."

She'd have to open her eyes soon, even though she knew now why she didn't want to. She didn't want to look at David.

Still another voice, calm and authoritative, said, "Hold it, everybody. I think she's coming around."

She lifted heavy eyelids. She was lying on the subway platform, with someone's folded overcoat under her head. The train, its doors closed, still stood in the station. Vaguely she was aware of curious and horrified faces peering from the windows.

The train's motorman, though, stood right beside her on the platform, looking down at her. A uniformed policeman was there, too, and the man in the green felt hat, and the other man—a fat man, she saw now, with thick-lensed glasses.

And David. His face was so strange, the skin a greenish-white, the pupils distended until his gray eyes looked almost black. He was frightened, terribly frightened. For her, or for himself?

The policeman said, "Don't talk unless you want to, miss.

66

You've had a bad shock. We've called an ambulance. It'll be here any minute."

"Hello, darling." David's lips had stretched themselves into a smile. "If you don't want the ambulance, just say so." He turned to the policeman. "I can take her to the hospital in a taxi."

Without knowing she was going to, she cried, "No!"

All the men stared down at her. She said wildly to David, "You just stay away from me! I don't want to ever see you again."

The policeman said in a subtly altered tone, "You want to make a charge against this man, miss? I mean, right now?"

"No."

"But if you think he pushed you—"

"I don't know whether he did or not." Closing her eyes, she turned her head away. "I just want him to go."

"All right," the policeman said soothingly, "he'll go. But first I have to make sure who he is, for my report. Mind showing me your driver's license or something, Mr. Bryant?"

8

When a sharp-featured nurse awoke her the next morning, Karen for a few hazy moments had the impression that she'd been for a long horseback ride after months of not riding at all. Her whole body, from the back of her neck to her ankles, had the muscular ache which comes after an unaccustomed hour or so in the saddle.

Then she remembered. Scream of brakes and glare of headlight, and David's green-white face looking down at her.

"How do you feel, Miss Wentworth?"

After a moment Karen answered, "Not bad, except that I feel stiff all over."

"That's from shock. Every muscle in your body must have tightened up. But you'll feel better after breakfast. And we're going to discharge you before lunch."

Karen tried to smile, and found that even her facial muscles were stiff. "Expecting another guest for this bed?"

"We always are. But that's not why we're booting you out. You're fine, except for a few scrapes and bruises."

And a memory that would be the stuff of future nightmares.

"Is it all right if I make some phone calls after a while?"

"Go right ahead." The nurse moved toward the room's other bed, partially hidden by a screen. "How's the leg?" Karen heard her ask. A woman's voice murmured something, and the nurse replied, "Well, if you must ski—"

Since she knew her landlady was an early riser, Karen phoned her immediately, explained that she'd had "a slight accident" in the subway, and asked the shocked and sympathetic Mrs. Orford to feed Bozo and then turn him out into the courtyard for a while. After breakfast she phoned her boss. Despite his obvious dismay that she wouldn't be in, he urged her to get a "gude rast, and slip a lot" over the weekend, and not come in Monday unless she felt "badder." After that she called Bill Bailey's office. He wasn't expected in until later, she was told, but he'd be given her message. Then, still feeling drowsy from the sedative she'd been given the night before, she took Mr. Bokarski's advice and went back to sleep.

Around ten the nurse awoke her. "Young man to see you," she said, and went out.

Stomach knotting with apprehension, Karen stared at the room's double half-doors. But it was Bill Bailey who came in. Grasping the back of the visitor's chair in one big hand, he brought it near the bed, sat down, and asked without preamble, "What happened?"

"I'm really not sure." As she recounted the episode in the subway, she saw his scowl deepen, and shock and anger gather in his blue eyes.

"You going to have this Bryant arrested?"

"No, I refused to enter charges. After all, Bill, it could have been an accident." Again she saw David's terrified face, and his hand reaching down to pull her to safety. But would he have reached down if he hadn't seen those two men come through the turnstiles onto the platform? Oh, surely he would have. It just couldn't be that David—witty, handsome David, whom she'd loved—could have desired her death. And yet—

She said wretchedly, "I just don't want to be alone with him again, ever."

"And you damn well won't! But I do think you ought to

have him picked up."

She shook her head. How could she make such a charge against anyone, let alone David, when probably he was guilty of no more than momentary clumsiness?

Bill's gaze searched her face. "All right. But don't you think it's time you told me more about this David Bryant, and about whoever it is you think might have sent that telegram, and all the rest of it?"

She told him. That since last Monday night, even before she reached the group on the hill, there was something strange about them, something altered. Their coldness to her, and her meeting with Evelyn Krim the next day, and the vague suspicion about the girl murdered in the parking lot which had haunted her ever since.

"Did you mention the girl to Bryant yesterday evening?"

"Yes. He said the man who did it had confessed. He also said that he himself was up in Boston when it happened. I don't think he would have told me lies like that, not when I could check on them so easily."

Bill's voice was grim. "But if that train had hit you, you wouldn't have been able to check on anything, would you?"

Somehow she hadn't thought of that. She felt the blood drain from her face. Then she said, "But it seemed to me he was telling the truth. About the girl in the parking lot, I mean."

"Maybe. Maybe he's in the clear on that. Maybe it was something else you said last night that made him decide a subway accident would be a good idea."

She said after several seconds, "I can't remember saying anything else that might have—" Her voice trailed off.

"Karen, would you mind if I consult Frank Rossi about this? He's a client of mine. He and his wife boarded their setter with me last summer. He's also a city detective. He's on the narcotics squad now, but he used to be on homicide."

"Bill, I told you—"

"This will be completely unofficial. The point is, I re-

70

member that a girl was stabbed to death in the museum parking lot, but I don't recall that the murderer had been caught. Frank can check on that—unofficially, mind you—in a couple of minutes. He can also check to see if anything else of the sort happened in the park about that time."

Why, that was what she'd said to David! She'd told him that she'd thought of going down to the *Times* to look up stories about that girl, and about anything else that might have happened in the park around the holidays or shortly thereafter.

"Yes," she said, "ask your friend to check."

Her tone brought a quizzical look to his eyes, but all he said was, "Okay. Now how about dinner tonight?"

The nurse pushed the swinging doors apart. "Time to get dressed, Miss Wentworth," she said, and disappeared.

Bill got to his feet. "Okay if I pick you up around six-thirty?"

"You might have to pick me up literally and carry me. I mean, I wouldn't like to go hobbling into a restaurant."

"You won't have to," he said after a moment. "I'll drop by around six-thirty. Bozo and I will take a walk over to that First Avenue place that sells casserole dinners to take out. I'll spoon-feed you, if you like. You won't have to move a muscle, except to open your mouth."

She smiled. Already, smiling hurt less. "That won't be necessary. In fact, I'll probably be pretty much okay in a few hours. But thanks for the thought."

An hour later, when Mrs. Orford opened the door to her ground-floor apartment, Karen said quickly, "Hold Bozo!"

Mrs. Orford caught the dog's collar, checking his joyous rush toward his owner. "I've got bruises," Karen explained.

"Oh, you poor child!" She hauled the dog to one side. "I've made some of my vegetable soup for your lunch. It's been simmering all morning." Mrs. Orford regarded her vegetable soup as a sovereign remedy for human woes, from influenza to melancholia.

Seated across from her landlady at the kitchen table, and with Bozo crowded against her leg, Karen described how she'd "slipped and fallen" from a subway platform. Because of Mrs. Orford's heart condition, Karen had decided to tell her no more than that.

Even so, the older woman's face had turned white. "If a train had come along, you might have been—" Then: "Was David hurt, too?" Mrs. Orford had met—and admired—David Bryant.

"No, he's all right."

"That reminds me. He sent you candy. At least I suppose it's from him. I found the box in front of my door about an hour ago." Rising, she took a box, wrapped in pink-and-silver-striped paper and tied with a silver ribbon, from the top of the refrigerator and laid it beside Karen's plate.

Karen stared down at the familiar wrapping paper. Marzipan, undoubtedly, from that shop two blocks away on Eighty-sixth Street. Throat tightening, she remembered how happy she'd been, last Christmas down in Raleigh, when the book of Renoir prints and a box of her favorite candy had arrived. A much bigger box. This one looked to be only a pound.

"There's a card with your name on the envelope," Mrs. Orford pointed out.

Karen drew the little envelope from beneath the wrapping paper's fold. In inked block letters it said, "Miss Karen Wentworth." Probably a delivery boy had left it out in the hall. But that was an odd thing for him to do. For David it would have been even odder.

Unless, she thought, her throat tightening up again, he'd felt just too wretched to face Mrs. Orford. She pictured him placing it there, with the idea that it would be safer than outside her own empty apartment. She pictured him turning away, walking swiftly but with shoulders drooping toward the street door.

Remembering her manners, she started to untie the silver

72

ribbon. "You like marzipan, don't you, Mrs. Orford?"

"Yes, but it doesn't like me. No sweets seem to, lately. Karen, why don't you go upstairs to bed? What you need, now that you've had your vegetable soup, is a nice long nap."

"I think you're right." She snapped Bozo's leash to his collar, thanked Mrs. Orford for lunch, and then, carrying the box of candy, went upstairs.

But she didn't go to bed. Sitting in the room's only armchair, she opened the little envelope. Also printed in block letters, the message on the card read, "Hoping for forgiveness."

From David, undoubtedly. But why had he printed the message? Well, maybe someone in the shop had. Maybe he'd ordered the candy and dictated the message over the phone. Still, it was such an odd message. In view of her wild cry of "Stay away from me!" the night before, why hadn't he written, "With the hope you'll change your mind," or, "Darling, you're wrong about me." This way, it sounded as if he were confessing to something. Perhaps, though, he'd meant only, "Forgive me for being clumsy." Yes, that must be what he'd meant. But in his upset state, he'd been unable to express himself with his usual ease.

She untied the box, laid ribbon and wrapping on the low table beside her chair, and lifted the lid. A single layer of fruit-shaped little candies inside. Rosy marzipan apples, tiny orange pumpkins with green stems, yellow bananas realistically flecked with brown.

Whining eagerly as the delicious smell of candy reached him, Bozo crossed the room and sat down in front of her, eyes fixed on her face. Usually Karen denied his insatiable sweet tooth everything except a brand of confections—Pupsickles, they were called—especially made for dogs. But every now and then she allowed him a piece of candy or half a cookie. "Well, just one," she said, and picked up a tiny pumpkin by its stem.

Its little cup of fluted green paper had stuck to it. Pulling the paper free, she dropped the candy into Bozo's expectant jaws.

Then, with a swift intake of breath, she leaned forward and slapped the side of his head. The little pumpkin popped out of his mouth onto the carpet.

9

With hurt, puzzled eyes the dog watched her as she retrieved the candy from the floor, dropped it into the box
lid, and then placed both halves of the box atop her tall,
narrow bookcase, out of his reach.

Lately, Bozo's had indeed been a dog's life. He'd been
loaded into a crate and flown through bumpy air. Then a
few days later a strange woman had led him away from Mrs.
Orford to someplace where another woman had shut him up
in a cage. It had seemed an eternity before Karen showed
up. She'd left him alone all last night. And now she'd
slapped candy out of his mouth just as he was about to
crunch down.

Standing beside the bookcase, Karen lifted a little banana
from its paper cup. Yes, on its underside it, too, had a tiny
hole. She'd noticed the hole as she pulled the paper away
from the first piece of candy, but it hadn't really registered
upon her consciousness until after she'd dropped the little
pumpkin into Bozo's mouth.

With fingers that were no longer quite steady, she took
every piece of candy in the box out of its paper cup, and
then replaced it. Many of the candies had stuck to the paper,
and no wonder, because each one, apparently, had been
pierced with something that left a tiny round hole.

Did it mean anything? Perhaps not. Perhaps all marzipan

from that shop, including the candy David had sent at Christmas, had similar holes. Maybe she just hadn't noticed before. Or perhaps, in recent weeks, the shop had decided to gild the lily by injecting some additional flavoring into the center of each confection.

The phone rang.

It was Bill. "How you feeling?"

"Better."

'That's good. Karen, my friend Frank Rossi just called me back. He checked on the case of that girl killed in the parking lot. A week after it happened, her common-law husband confessed. It's an open-and-shut case. He hadn't even got rid of the knife that made the wounds. So I guess your friend Bryant is in the clear on that one."

With the phone held to her ear, Karen stared at the candy box atop the bookcase. "Yes," she said.

"Frank's up to his ears in narcotic squad business right now. But as soon as he can, probably first thing tomorrow, he's going to check to see what else Bryant and your park friends might have got mixed up in around Christmas or early in January. Even if he doesn't get to it until day after tomorrow, we'll get information a lot faster than if we tried to look it up ourselves."

"Yes," Karen said again. Then, with a rush: "Bill, someone sent me a box of marzipan. I think it was David, although the card's unsigned, and printed rather than written. Whoever it was just left the box in the hall, outside my landlady's door."

His voice was sharp. "Have you eaten any of it?"

"No, and I'm not going to. There's—there's a tiny little hole in each piece—"

"Put the box away! Under lock and key, if you can."

She looked at her rosewood desk, its small brass key projecting from the drawer lock. The desk, a present from her parents on her fourteenth birthday, was the only furniture

76

beside the bookcase she'd had sent up from Raleigh. "I can lock it up."

"Have you saved the wrapping?"

"Yes, but I don't see how that will do much good, or the box either. The people in the shop have handled it, and so have I. And Mrs. Orford's prints must be on the wrapping."

"It still might show something. Handle it as little as possible when you put it away. And save the card, of course."

"All right." She paused. "Bill, then you think the candy's been—tampered with?"

"How can we know until it's analyzed? Karen, I'll get over there before six-thirty if I possibly can. Right now we've got trouble on our hands here."

"What's the matter?"

"One of the dog walkers just reported that a German shepherd we've been boarding bit a boy of about ten in the park. It wasn't a bad bite, just a finger, and the kid ran off before the dog walker could stop him. Now we're trying to locate the owner—he's down in Florida—to make sure the shepherd's had rabies shots. If we can't locate him soon, we'll have to broadcast an alarm, so that the kid's parents will take him to a doctor for shots."

Her own concerns momentarily forgotten, she said, "Oh, Bill! I do hope that dog isn't rabid."

"The chances are a hundred to one against it. There hasn't been a case of rabies in Manhattan for many years. But of course we can't take even that one chance. Now about you—"

"Don't worry about me."

"What do you mean, don't worry? Of course I worry. But if you'll just sit tight until I get there—"

"I will."

"I'd suggest you hand the box over to the police right now, except that we'll get the results faster if we let Frank Rossi handle it. I read in the paper that police poison lab has so much work it's weeks behind."

"Yes, better to let him handle it. And I'll see you at six-thirty or thereabout."

When she'd hung up, she gathered the candy box from the bookcase, and the wrapping and ribbon and card from the table beside the armchair. Handling them as gingerly as possible, she carried them to the desk and locked them inside its drawer. Then, after a moment's hesitation, she took the key out of the lock, crossed the room, and dropped the key into a blue lusterware bowl that sat atop the bookcase.

Turning, she stared at the desk. It seemed to her now that the chances were overwhelming that the candy was all right. Even if David had shoved her intentionally off that platform —and she was by no means sure he had—would he make another attempt on her life so soon? After all, the police had a record of the subway incident, including David's name and address. That meant that if she met with any other sort of suspicious mishap, David would be the first suspect. No, if David had bought that candy, it must be all right.

If David had bought it. But what if someone else had placed the candy in front of Mrs. Orford's apartment this morning and then scurried along the hall to the street door?

She shivered, there in the warm, silent apartment, and looked uneasily around at the familiar furniture, at Bozo lying with his muzzle on his extended paws and with eyes rolled reproachfully up at her. Though the thought of David leaving poisoned candy for her had been repugnant and frightening, she felt even more chilled by the thought that some other person—faceless, nameless as yet—might be seeking her death.

It came back to her then, the feeling that had assailed her the other night on the hill, that cold, inexplicable sense that each of those people up there felt threatened by her presence, and therefore hostile to her.

"Oh, for heaven's sake!" she said aloud. Until now, in her

78

distraught state, she hadn't stopped to consider that there might be a quick and simple way of learning who'd bought the candy. The sweetshop was only two blocks away.

"Come on, Bozo," she said. "We're going for a walk."

10

The temperature, which had struggled up almost to freezing earlier that day, had now dropped back into the low twenties. Along Eighty-sixth Street, the main shopping thoroughfare of the German neighborhood known as Yorkville, pedestrians moved briskly, muffled to their cold-reddened ears. Karen passed a German-language bookstore, a café with a window poster showing a photograph of entertainers in Bavarian costume, and then stopped before the sweetshop. After a moment's hesitation, she tied Bozo's leash to a parking meter. She'd be able to keep an eye on him through the broad display window.

The shop, which drew patrons from all over Manhattan, was as always very crowded. Behind the counter three harried-looking women in pink uniforms and white ruffled caps served the customers lined up before them. Karen joined the line served by the woman she knew was the manager, a tall, heavy-featured brunette of about thirty-five. When at last it was her turn, Karen said swiftly, "I wonder if you could tell me if you delivered a box of candy to my apartment house today."

"Name?"

"Karen Wentworth." She added her address.

Turning to a clipboard that hung on the wall, the woman leafed through a sheaf of white paper slips. "Not today," she said, turning back.

Unhappily aware of the lengthening line behind her, Karen said, "Then I wonder if you remember a blond man of about thirty buying a pound of marzipan today. His hair's a pale yellow, and he's tall, over six feet. Gray-eyed, very good-looking—"

As Karen spoke, the impatience in the manager's eyes had given way to a reminiscent look. "He wasn't in here today. But just before Christmas he bought a three-pound box of marzipan and asked us to send it to someone in North Carolina."

"He sent it to me."

The woman said with ironical envy, "Well, lucky you. But he hasn't been in here today. If he had been, I'd have remembered." She looked past Karen's shoulder to the woman next in line.

Karen said hurriedly, "I'll take a half pound of those," and pointed to an assortment of chocolate creams directly in front of her on the glass-enclosed counter. As the woman began, with lightning speed, to place candies in a half-pound box, Karen added, "Do you remember a middle-aged man, rather heavy-set, buying a pound of marzipan today?" That description would fit either George Kinsing or Henry Maize. "Or maybe it was a brunette woman, short and rather plump, quite pretty—"

"Look!" the manager said explosively. "Just look around you. It's like this all day, every day. I remembered your boy friend because—well, I just did. But those other people you're talking about, they'd have to have two heads before I remembered them." She tightened the silver bow with a vicious jerk of her fingers, and thrust the wrapped box at Karen. "That'll be ninety cents, please."

Reaching into her red shoulder bag, Karen noticed that one end of its strap had been torn partially loose. It must have happened, she reflected fleetingly, when David and the other man had pulled her up to the subway platform. She

81

paid the woman and turned away.

Out on the sidewalk, Karen found that the short winter day had faded into dusk. She untied Bozo and then just stood there, indecisively, at the curb's edge.

So David hadn't left that marzipan, whether poisoned or unpoisoned, outside Mrs. Orford's door. And if he'd made no attempt upon her life today, probably he hadn't last night, either.

But wait a minute. The manager might not have been behind the counter all morning. Without remembering it now, she might have gone back to the lavatory. Or, since this was Friday, she might have taken the week's receipts to the bank, as many neighborhood shopkeepers did. In the interval, David might have come in and bought the marzipan.

And if not David, who? Who had left the candy with its odd, hand-printed message? Again she had that impression of another shadowy someone, frightened of her, and therefore determinedly hostile.

Then, turning east, she moved decisively down the street, with Bozo trotting ahead of her. She'd call on May Cosgrove, who lived in the next block. Almost from the first she'd been aware that Mrs. Cosgrove was—well, eccentric. But she'd liked her, and the serene-faced little widow had obviously returned her liking. Perhaps Mrs. Cosgrove would have some idea of who might have sent the candy.

Below First Avenue, she stopped at an old brownstone sandwiched in between a furniture warehouse and a Lutheran church. The vestibule held no intercom, but just two rows of bells with names beside them. She rang Mrs. Cosgrove's bell, waited until an answering buzz told her that the door latch had been released, and then walked back along a musty, dimly lit hall to a flight of descending stairs.

11

When Mrs. Cosgrove opened her door to see Karen standing there in the basement hall, with her aureole—such a pretty one; violet—hovering above her head, she at first thought she faced a ghost. Then she became aware of the dog.

It was most unlikely that the dog would have passed on, too. Responsible people didn't feed candy to their pets, and Karen had always struck her as a responsible young person. Of course, if the dog *had* passed on, his spirit might very well be accompanying that of his mistress. One of the several points of Christian doctrine with which Mrs. Cosgrove had come to disagree was that pertaining to souls. Surely souls weren't restricted to humans. She had no doubt that she and her Sistie had met in past lives, and would do so again in future ones.

"Why, hello, dear."

"Hello, Mrs. Cosgrove. I know I shouldn't drop in like this, but—"

"Not at all, dear; not at all." She opened the door wide. "I'm always pleased to have company."

When the girl and her dog walked in, Sistie's true-to-form reaction erased any lingering doubt that both visitors were alive. In fact here on her home ground Sistie was even more autocratic than usual. For perhaps half a minute, growling deep in her throat, she kept Bozo in his abjectly supine position, until Mrs. Cosgrove said, "That's enough, Sistie. Bozo's your guest." Then, to the girl: "Please sit down, dear."

Sitting down, Karen placed the flat package she'd been carrying on a little marble-topped table beside her, one of the many small tables, all bearing ornaments and photographs, in the crowded room. It wasn't until then that Mrs. Cosgrove noticed that the wrapping paper was pink and silver. For a startled moment she thought it was the box of marzipan. But no. The box beside the girl was a half-pound one, and she'd bought a full pound.

"Been buying candy, dear?"

"Yes, chocolate creams. Would you like some?"

"No, thank you. I never eat sweets."

Now why should the girl buy chocolates when she had a whole pound of her favorite candy, marzipan? Mrs. Cosgrove knew it was Karen's favorite because David, one night on the hill, had mentioned that it was.

Could it be that the girl had never received the marzipan? Could someone else have appropriated it as it lay there outside the manager's door—some delivery boy, or another tenant, or the manager herself? Mrs. Cosgrove hoped not; she most fervently hoped not.

She'd tried to be as careful about that as she could, under the circumstances. Still undecided as to just where to leave the candy, she'd carried it around to Karen's apartment house. In the vestibule, she'd decided to ring the apartment bell of a Mrs. Gerard on the fifth floor, in the hope that Mrs. Gerard was at home and would release the catch on the front door without first demanding through the intercom to know who the visitor was. With her gloved finger ready to push the button, she noticed that the front door already stood slightly ajar. (People were so careless these days, even though everyone knew there was so much crime and violence about.) She'd slipped into the lower hall. As she moved quietly down it, she saw, beside a door, a card bearing the word "Manager." Radio or TV music came from behind it. Hesitating there, she'd also heard Bozo's familiar bark. So he'd caught her scent. That had decided her. The box would be much safer there than outside Karen's silent, empty apartment. Anyone stooping to pick up the candy would probably change his mind when he heard the dog's warning bark. She'd left the box and slipped quietly away.

"Shall I make us some tea, dear?"

"Oh, please don't bother. I mustn't stay long." She was looking at the small table beside Mrs. Cosgrove's rocking chair. On it was a silver-framed newspaper photograph of David and the stub of a candle in a blue china holder. She was not surprised by the photograph. She'd been aware that the gentle old lady fervently admired David. But for a moment the candle stub puzzled her. Then the probable explanation came to her. A fuse must have blown out recently. While waiting for the superintendent to install a new one, Mrs. Cosgrove had sat there with a lighted candle beside her.

May Cosgrove followed the direction of Karen's gaze. "It's quite a good likeness, I thought, for a newspaper picture. Aren't we fortunate to have someone so brilliant and talented in our little group? So very, very fortunate."

"Yes." Karen's voice was constrained.

"Dear, something's bothering you, isn't it?"

"Yes," Karen said again, and then blurted out, "I think someone sent me poisoned candy."

At moments of crisis, Mrs. Cosgrove had learned, it was best to give whatever response her instinct dictated. "Poisoned!" she said.

Where had she made her mistake? She'd tried to be so careful. In the kitchen, wearing her white silk summer gloves, she'd taken each piece in turn from its paper cup. After all, she hadn't known which pieces the girl would select, or, for that matter, how much insecticide would be required to—to accomplish what was necessary. Using the hypodermic needle which had helped ease her poor husband's distress during has last weeks on earth, she'd deposited a few drops at the heart of each candy. The puncture marks had been small and neat. Still wearing the silk gloves, she'd put the pieces back in the box, rewrapped it in its pretty paper, and tied the silver ribbon into a bow. Then, on the blank card provided by the sweetshop, she'd printed her message. And she'd meant it. She did hope that the girl, once she reached the astral plane, would forgive her, just as she hoped that the insecticide would cause little or no suffering. After all, she felt no malice toward Karen. In fact, she liked her. But unfortunately Karen, by her insistence last Tuesday night on her right to come to any part of the park at any time she chose, had made it imperative that she be removed permanently.

Mrs. Cosgrove asked, "What made you think it was poisoned? Did it taste odd?" She'd been aware of that hazard. But after all, only a few drops in the midst of all that almond paste, and sugar, and artificial flavoring, and heaven knew what all. Anyway, very bad for the teeth. It was pride in her own teeth, most of which were still those nature had given her, which made her reject candy in all its forms.

"No," Karen said, "I didn't eat any of it. You see, I noticed there was a tiny hole in each piece." Her voice became uncertain. "Of course, maybe marzipan is always like that. Maybe they add extra flavoring that way." She glanced at the box of chocolate creams beside her. Now she realized that she should have bought marzipan, so that she could make an immediate comparison. But upset by the manager's impatience, and wanting to placate her, she'd pointed to the first candy her gaze fell upon.

"Mrs. Cosgrove, have you ever noticed whether or not marzipan has puncture marks?"

"I told you, dear, that I never eat sweets." Which, of course, was the truth. "What did you do with the candy?" If the girl had left it lying around, some innocent person

86

might . . .

"I put it away in my desk and locked the drawer. Bozo's so crazy about candy that he might try to claw the drawer open."

"Well, if you think there's something wrong with it, wouldn't it be wiser to flush all of it away?"

"Perhaps." Eager to get on with her questions, Karen didn't argue the point. "Mrs. Cosgrove, have you noticed anything odd about the Kinsings, and Henry Maize, and the others?"

"Odd?"

"They used to be friendly. But now it's plain they don't want anything to do with me. Why, I'm convinced that one of them sent that wire about Bozo the other day as—as sort of a warning not to come to the hill."

Mrs. Cosgrove's instincts furnished her no reply to that, and so she made none. She had arranged for Bozo's temporary and harmless removal as a warning. But it had proved ineffectual. And now this fiasco of the marzipan . . .

"Mrs. Cosgrove, did something—happen while I was away?"

Mrs. Cosgrove looked long and thoughtfully at the girl. And suddenly the truth came to her. She, May Cosgrove, had been in error.

Because Karen might well have represented a threat to David, Mrs. Cosgrove had assumed that she was an innocent instrument of the forces of evil. But was that the case? After all, the two young people from the first had been interested in each other—more than interested. With pleasure, Mrs. Cosgrove had heard them refer to evenings they'd spent together, and had observed the soft look in Karen's hazel eyes when they rested on David. As she'd remarked last fall to that rather awful Doris Kinsing—who, of course, hadn't liked it—they might all be invited to a wedding soon.

And so why hadn't she realized that Karen, too, if she knew the truth, would want to protect David? Why had she assumed that because of her youth the girl wouldn't have the largeness of soul to act on the plane of the higher morality, rather than in accordance with manmade laws?

Yes, her assumption had been wrong. Because of it, she'd twice taken active steps to ensure removal of what she regarded as the girl's threatening presence. Twice she'd failed. And that, plainly, was a sign.

"Yes, dear," she said quietly, "Something tragic happened while you were away. With no intent or desire to do so, David took a human life."

After several seconds, Karen managed to move her lips. "Who?"

"A complete stranger. A harmless, elderly man who ran a bookstore on Second Avenue."

"A stranger." Karen felt numb bewilderment. "Then why—?"

"David thought he was something else. A thoroughly evil man, a dope addict and would-be extortionist. You see, it was snowing that night, and it was dark, of course. It's no wonder that David mistook that poor man for"—her lips twisted with distaste—"Slide Thompson."

"Slide!"

"A nickname, undoubtedly. He's a jazz musician, a trombonist. David naturally assumed it was this Thompson coming toward him, because he'd arranged to meet him there. And when he saw the other man reach inside his coat, he took out his own gun. He didn't intend to fire it, and doesn't even remember pulling the trigger. It was—"

"Excuse me, Mrs. Cosgrove, but hadn't you better tell it from the beginning?"

"That would be better, wouldn't it? Well, it happened the tenth of last January. It had started snowing about an hour before I left the apartment with Sistie, and by the time I reached the hill, it was really coming down. I didn't mind, of course. The park is so beautiful when snow is falling. Only Paul Winship and the Kinsings were there when I arrived, but very soon David and his sister showed up, and right after them, Henry Maize."

They'd all chatted for a while. Then David, as he so often did, had taken Britt to the playing field deeper in the park.

"He'd been gone only a few minutes when we heard brakes squealing on that automobile road near where we meet. Henry said, 'Oh, my God!' The snow was too thick for us to see what had made the car put on its brakes, but Henry had looked around and seen that his old cocker spaniel was missing, and right away he was sure Fluff had wandered onto the road. Maybe you remember her doing that twice last fall."

Concealing her impatience, Karen said, "I remember."

"Well, Henry hurried away toward the road. The snow was falling so thickly by then that after he'd gone about fifteen feet, it just seemed to swallow him up. As it turned out, Fluff had got safely across the road, but of course we didn't know that then."

With snow falling in thick curtains all around them, they'd waited for Henry. When he finally returned, he not only had Fluff with him, but David and the Great Dane as well.

"Even before we could see them, we knew something was terribly wrong. We heard David breathing in a hoarse, labored way, almost like sobbing. Then we saw them. David was sort of stumbling through the snow, leaning against Henry's shoulder. Henry was leading the spaniel, but Britt was just following along behind, trailing her leash. His sister ran to David and shook his arm and said, 'David! What is it?' It wasn't until then that I saw that his right hand was hanging loosely at his side, with a gun in it. He said, 'God help me, God help me. I just killed a man.' "

While the others listened in numb silence, he'd gone on talking, sometimes haltingly, sometimes in a rush of words. About a year before, he'd said, he'd been a guest on a TV talk show. In the orchestra had been a hophead trombonist

89

named Slide Thompson, who'd been filling in for the band's regular trombonist. Thompson had asked David for "a ten-spot," and David, feeling sorry for him, had handed over the money.

"Perhaps," Mrs. Cosgrove said, "that gave the creature the idea that David was a person easily imposed upon. Anyway, he began calling up, accusing David of having had him blacklisted from future jobs on that particular show, and making all sorts of vague threats. At first David tried to reason with him. Later, as the man became more abusive, David just hung up on him whenever he called. Finally, though, this Thompson person called and suggested in a very conciliatory way that they meet to talk things over. Hoping to argue the man out of his obsession, David agreed. What's more, he offered to pay the man two hundred dollars in return for a written statement that he withdrew his absurd charges, and would make no more trouble."

Thompson had promptly accepted the offer, but when David suggested that Thompson come to his apartment, the man had turned cagey. Nor would he agree to meet in a bar or restaurant.

"Apparently," Mrs. Cosgrove said, "the creature was afraid David would have police officers stationed to arrest him for extortion, which heaven knows is what the poor boy should have done. But instead he suggested that they meet for a few minutes in Central Park. Thompson agreed to that.

"David had ample reason to fear the man might be dangerous. And so, along with the two hundred dollars, he brought a gun with him to the park that night. It was a small gun, a twenty-two, I believe they call it, which had been among the things he'd inherited from his father."

Leaving his little group of friends, David had walked away with Britt through the swirling snow to the agreed-upon meeting place, the far end of a playing field used for sand-lot baseball and football. He'd waited there for several minutes, growing more and more nervous and apprehensive.

Finally he saw a man's dark figure moving toward him. He saw, or thought he saw, the man reach inside his coat, as if for a gun. Reaching swiftly into the pocket of his duffel coat, David brought out his gun.

"And then somehow, Karen dear, the gun went off, not once but several times. David saw the man fall. Henry Maize saw it, too. He'd just found Fluff and was leading her back to us when he became aware of two men standing only a few yards away. Even through the snowflakes, he recognized one of them as David. His height, you know, and that pale blond hair. Then he saw flashes of light, and sounds that, as Henry later said, were like small exploding firecrackers. Then the other man fell."

Henry had hurried over. He and David, who seemed dazed with shock, had knelt beside the fallen man. It wasn't until Henry lit his cigarette lighter, David later told them, that he realized he'd shot a complete stranger. He was an elderly man, and very thin.

"Henry felt for the man's pulse, and listened for a heartbeat. Finally he had to tell David that the man was dead."

Supported by Henry, David had made his way back to the group. "And there, with all of us around him, he told us what had happened."

Mrs. Cosgrove stopped speaking. Karen asked in a thin voice, "And then?"

"Well, dear, it was then that Consuelo turned to all of us. She really looked—quite fierce. She said, 'It was an accident! All of you must see that. You must give David and me a chance to think what to do. At least promise me that you'll keep quiet about this for twenty-four hours.' "

Karen looked dazedly at the serene old face. "And all of you did promise?"

"Well, dear, of course. Doris Kinsing said right away that she wouldn't dream of telling the police. Then she turned on her husband in that highhanded way of hers—I really don't care for that woman!—and said, 'You'd better promise, too, George. You'd *better.*' And after a moment he said he would. Henry also promised. He looked quite sick and shaken, poor man, perhaps as much so as David. Then Paul Winship—you know the silly way he talks—said something like, 'Since we're fellow composers, man, you can count on me not to buzz the fuzz.' I, of course, felt no hesitation in promising. It *was* an accident. But unfortunately it was one which, if it came to light, might ruin David's whole future. And he has a future more exalted than anyone realizes." But me, she added mentally.

She hesitated. Should she tell the girl that she was the one who had reached out her hand and said, "I'll get rid of the gun for you, David?" No, she decided. In the first place, it would sound like boasting. In the second, she'd told no one so far, not even David, of her little secret about the privet bush. When he'd asked what she'd done with the gun, she replied that it was better for him not to know, and to just forget all about it.

"Who did you say the man was that David—?"

How pale the poor girl looked! Well, naturally, it was a great shock to her, considering how she felt about David. "He was a secondhand bookseller named Herman Dockweiler, an immigrant from Australia. He and his wife ran a shop near here on Second Avenue. We all learned that from the newspapers the next day. Not the *Times.* It comes out in the morning, and the body wasn't discovered until after daylight, half buried in snow. But the later editions of the *Post* carried the story. The police were baffled, the papers said. Because of the half-frozen condition of the body, the time of death couldn't be set any closer than between six in the evening and midnight. The snow had covered up any footprints there might have been, and there seemed to be no motive. The poor man still had his wallet on him, with almost a hundred dollars in it. And his wife said he had no enemies."

The steampipes overhead made a shuddering sound, and

then gave a series of knocks. With a slight frown, Mrs. Cosgrove glanced upward. In view of the last voluntary rent increase she'd granted him, her landlord should have done something about those pipes. After all, there was such a thing as keeping your pledged word. Then she lowered her gaze to her guest and said, "The newspapers also reported that his doctor had given Mr. Dockweiler only a few months to live. Perhaps that influenced the decision of the others to keep silent. After all, poor Mr. Dockweiler had had nothing ahead of him but a painful death."

Karen asked, in a numb voice, "Didn't the police question any of you?"

"Of course, dear. You know that motor scooter policeman, the one who often comes by on that asphalt path that runs behind the museum? Well, he knew who David was, from seeing him on TV, and I suppose he reported that David and the rest of us might have heard or seen something when the poor man was killed. Anyway, detectives came to David, and he told them the story we'd all agreed upon—I mean, that we'd heard and seen nothing, which I'm sure didn't strike the police as strange, considering that the playing field is a quarter of a mile from where we gather. And, of course, falling snow muffles sound. The detectives asked for the names of the rest of our little group, and each of us was visited that afternoon."

The one who'd visited her, Mrs. Cosgrove recalled, had been very nice. She'd told him how the landlord had failed to do anything about those noisy pipes, and the detective had seemed sympathetic, even indignant. What she should do, he told her, was to haul her landlord into court.

Karen said, in that same numb voice, "And no one else has come forward as a witness?"

"No, dear. It's extremely unlikely that there were any witnesses besides Henry. It was pitch dark at that hour, and the snowfall was heavy. Not at all the sort of night for a stroll through the park, or anywhere else. Besides, the spot where David had agreed to meet that Thompson creature was a good many yards off the path—near the playing field backstop, as I understand it."

"And you and the Kinsings and the others have gone on meeting in the park each night?"

"Of course. The police might have thought it odd if we'd stopped doing so."

"And for almost a month you've all kept silent?"

"That's right, dear."

Karen thought dazedly, "Why?" Why had all six of them agreed to remain silent about the slaying, however accidental, of another human being? Oh, she could certainly understand why David's sister had wanted to protect him, and why Doris Kinsing had, too. And considering that Paul Winship was one of life's hitchhikers, so to speak, trying to ride to fame and fortune by means of another man's talent, it wasn't surprising that he'd jumped at the chance to make the owner of that talent beholden to him. But why had George Kinsing and Henry Maize, two respectable, middle-aged men, jeopardized their reputations, their jobs, and perhaps even their freedom by remaining silent? She had no idea why. She only knew that they obviously had.

As for May Cosgrove, Karen thought, looking at her hostess's gentle face, the woman plainly idolized David.

"It's hard to understand," Karen said, "why at least one of them—Henry, say, or George Kinsing—hasn't changed his mind and gone to the police."

It wasn't hard for Mrs. Cosgrove to understand. It was obvious to her that all those others, even in their unenlightened state, had some dim consciousness of David's true greatness. No matter what other motives they thought they had, that was the compelling one.

Mrs. Cosgrove said, "It shouldn't be too hard for you to understand, Karen dear. I mean, it's been obvious to me that you loved David." She tipped her white curly head archly to one side. "Or was I mistaken about that?"

"No," Karen said, after a moment, "you weren't mistaken."

"In that case, you'll be as eager as any of us to protect David."

"I don't know," Karen said wretchedly. "I don't know."

For a fleeting instant she saw in the woman's eyes something that chilled her. Then Mrs. Cosgrove smiled.

"You'll protect him, dear." Of course the girl would. Otherwise why had she been given a sign to tell Karen everything?

Gathering up her purse and the box of chocolate creams, Karen stood up. "I'd better go now. I've—" She broke off. She'd been about to say, with automatic politeness, "I've enjoyed my visit." Bending to Bozo, who sat companionably haunch-to-haunch with Sistie, she snapped his leash onto his collar.

Mrs. Cosgrove asked, "Will we see you in the park tonight, dear?"

The woman was strange, Karen reflected—very strange. From her placid manner one would have thought they'd spent the past hour discussing flower arrangements. "I—I don't think so. I'll be busy."

"Well, anyway, we'll be seeing each other soon."

12

On the brownstone's front steps, Karen stood motionless for perhaps two minutes. It was fully dark now. Not really seeing them, she stared at the people hurrying past, that tired, end-of-the-day look on their faces.

How could she keep silent? A murder—or at least an accidental homicide had been committed, and she knew about it.

On the other hand, how could she be the one to turn David in?

She had a sudden memory of last New Year's Eve down in Raleigh. Despite the fact that he was still convalescent, her father had insisted that they follow their annual custom of giving a party, with the guests ranging in age from Karen's contemporaries to her parents'. Around eleven, David had called from New York, sounding so warm and tender that she was sure he'd soon ask her to marry him. After they'd said good night, she'd slipped up to her room to be alone for a few minutes. At the window, staring at a beech tree which spread its bare branches against a frostily brilliant night sky, she'd visualized their future, hers and David's. Growing success for him. A house in Connecticut within a few years. And children, two of them. Ideally, the boy would be born first, and, if it was all right with David, they'd name him Andrew. The girl would be Caroline, after

Karen's mother. They'd both be blond, of course, at least as small children. Karen's hair had been blond when she was small. And they'd be beautiful, so beautiful.

Only dream children, of course. And yet despite the fact that there'd been only one more phone call from David, followed by weeks of puzzling silence, small Andrew and Caroline had remained very real to her. They were real even now, when she knew that those particular children would never be born. How, therefore, could she be the one to turn David in?

And yet, and yet, David had killed another human being, however inadvertently.

Walking might help her to think more clearly. She went down the steps and, with Bozo beside her, turned east. As she passed the sweetshop, she saw that it was still open, and still crowded. But she wouldn't have gone in even if the shop had been empty of customers. The matter of the marzipan seemed to her comparatively unimportant now. And anyway, Bill Bailey's detective friend would have the candy analyzed the next day.

Bill. She mustn't tell Bill anything about the old man killed in the park, not until she had decided what to do about it. In the short time she'd known him, she'd learned that Bill was a man of direct, and swift, action. He'd say that the thing to do about a case of homicide was to put it in the hands of the homicide squad—and he'd probably be dialing the police as he said it. No, she wouldn't even risk seeing him tonight, lest he bully her into telling him the whole thing.

She glanced at her watch. After five. Before long, she'd better phone Bill and break their date.

The entrance to Carl Schurz Park lay just ahead. She turned off onto one of the paths sloping up toward Mayor Lindsay's house, and then unsnapped Bozo's leash. "Get yourself some exercise," she advised him. "You're not going to chase around with your dog friends on the hill tonight."

Almost as if he understood, he darted away through the leafless bushes.

She stood there, wretched with indecision, her booted feet turning cold on the icy path. There were several puzzling aspects to the story May Cosgrove had told her, she realized now. It was not only strange that two seemingly responsible men like Henry and George had kept silent. It was also strange that David himself hadn't gone immediately to the police. Surely that would have been preferable to the life he was leading now. She thought of him as he'd been at dinner last night and during their window-shopping along Second Avenue—charming, amusing, apparently without a serious care in the world. And yet a good deal of the time, in the back of his mind, there must have been the thought of that poor old man lying dead in the snow. What a strain living must be for him these days!

True, if he'd told the police about it, there'd have been a lot of publicity, and almost certainly a prison sentence. But probably it wouldn't have been a long one. Surely any judge, any jury, would understand why it might have been fearful enough to take a gun along to a meeting with someone like Slide Thompson.

Thompson. Why hadn't he met David that night? And in the weeks since then, had David heard from him? It seemed probable that a man of that sort, reading newspaper accounts of Herman Dockweiler's mysterious death, would have guessed the identity of the killer, and have demanded far more from David than two hundred dollars. Was that the case? She couldn't know. Mrs. Cosgrove had said nothing on that point.

Sudden realization made her draw in her breath. As far as she knew, the group on the hill had only David's word for it that such a person as Slide Thompson existed.

But surely he did, or had. Surely David must have thought it was Slide Thompson, dope addict and would-be extortionist, moving toward him through the snow, his hand reaching inside his overcoat. Otherwise, why would David even have taken out his gun? What motive could David possibly have had for killing the elderly proprietor of a secondhand bookstore?

Nevertheless, she forced herself to consider the possibility that David had lied to his friends. If he'd done that, if Thompson had no existence outside of David's quick and resourceful imagination, then the death of that old man probably hadn't been an accidental homicide, but cold-blooded murder. And she—in spite of the love she'd felt for David, and in spite of those two wistful, never-to-be-born dream children—would have to go to the police.

Try to find out first, she told herself. Try to find out if there really is a Slide Thompson.

But how? Even if he lived in Manhattan, as he probably did, he wouldn't be listed in the phone book as "Slide" Thompson. Nor could she call up every Thompson in the book. Manhattan probably held almost as many Thompsons as Smiths.

Perhaps, though, there was a way.

She called out "Bozo!" and heard branches crackle as he ran toward her.

A few minutes later, at a newsstand on the corner of Eighty-sixth Street and Third Avenue, she bought a copy of *Musicians' Digest,* and then walked to her apartment. As soon as she was inside the door, she phoned Bill Bailey's office. Mr. Bailey, a girl's voice told her, had gone up to his apartment. "But I can switch you over to his phone."

"No! Please don't. I'm in a hurry. Would you please just tell him that Karen Wentworth called to say she's sorry, but she can't see him this evening? Something's come up."

"All right, I'll tell him." The girl's tone had turned cool.

Probably, Karen thought, she admired her boss, and resented his being stood up.

"Thank you very much. Oh! One thing more. Did you find out about that German shepherd, the one that bit a

99

little boy?"

The girl's voice was still frosty. "We finally located the dog's owner down in Florida. He said he'd had the dog inoculated against rabies, and the vet whose name he gave us confirmed that."

"Oh, I'm so glad. Well, good-bye."

She fed Bozo after that. As for herself, she felt too tense to want dinner. Sitting down beside the phone, she opened *Musicians' Digest* to its masthead and scanned the list of staff members for unusual names. After that she looked up, and dialed, the numbers of a Drew Saperstein, a Sylvester Yuell, and a Canford Malek. Mr. Saperstein's phone was answered by an answering service, and Mr. Yuell's wasn't answered at all. But Mr. Malek was at home.

Karen said, "I wonder if you could give me some information. Have you ever heard of a jazz musician named Slide Thompson?"

"Thompson, Thompson. Oh, sure. He used to play trombone sometimes at Nick's down in the Village, years and years ago."

"Do you know how I could get in touch with him?"

"I wouldn't have the remotest. He may be dead, for all I know. Only thing I can suggest is that you call the Musicians' Union tomorrow."

"Thank you, but in the meantime, do you happen to know what his real first name is?"

"I never heard him called anything but Slide. But wait. Hold the phone. I've got a copy of *Who's Who in Jazz* around here someplace."

After an interval he said, "Got it. He was born Cuthbert Claude Thompson in Little Rock, Arkansas, in nineteen fourteen. Cuthbert Claude! No wonder he called himself Slide."

"Thank you. Thank you very much."

For a moment after she hung up, she just sat there staring at the little blue jar into which she'd dropped the desk key.

100

She felt an odd mixture of relief and intensified conflict. In one way she was glad to know that David hadn't lied, that he really had thought he was facing a perhaps dangerous man that night. In another way, she was sorry. If she'd been able to hang up feeling reasonably sure that David had lied, her dilemma would have been solved. No matter what emotional wrench it might have cost her, she'd have had to call the police.

And then she realized that her conversation with the magazine editor had proved only that there was, or had been, a trombonist named Slide Thompson. It hadn't proved that he and David had arranged to meet in the park that night. Slide Thompson's name might have been one that David, in his desperation, had snatched up out of his memory.

If she could just talk to this Thompson . . .

Swiftly she turned to the "T's" in the phone book. A C. C. Thompson lived on Fifth Avenue, and a C. Claude Thompson on West Forty-seventh Street. Since it was most unlikely that a broken-down trombonist would be living on Fifth Avenue, she dialed the second number. After three rings a man's voice said, "Hello."

"Excuse me, but I'm trying to locate a musician named Slide Thompson."

"You've got him. Now what can I do for you?"

13

George Kinsing thrust his gloved hands deeper into his overcoat pockets. Wasn't the cold ever to relent? This was the eighth straight day of sub-freezing temperatures. And now, with the heavily crusted snow of last week's fall still blanketing the park and lying in trash-studded heaps in the gutters, another snowstorm was moving eastward. It would reach the city around noon tomorrow, the weather bureau had predicted, and it would be a severe one, perhaps depositing even more snow than the big storm of last January tenth.

If only he could get away! Not just from New York, and this deep-freeze winter, and his enforced attendance at these ghastly little gatherings on the hill, but clear out of the country.

Well, David would probably go abroad soon. Almost a month had passed since the old man's death. If the police hadn't suspected David up until now, which they obviously hadn't, there wasn't much chance that his departure would attract their attention. As soon as David was gone, George would resign his job and take Doris to Europe for the rest of their lives. Some warm country—Italy, perhaps. Doris would like that, he reflected ironically. No place like Italy for a woman with a roving eye. And maybe he could find a job over there with some American firm. Not that he'd actually need the money. He had enough put by. But he'd hate to be idle, in Italy or anywhere else.

True, he'd be trying to run away from himself, and people said you couldn't do that. But maybe you could. Maybe on the other side of the Atlantic, he'd feel less weighted by the knowledge that he'd botched the entire last twenty-five years of his life, starting with the day he married Doris and ending with what he was now, a supposedly respectable businessman who was keeping quiet about a murder.

No, he corrected himself, not murder. A homicide, an accidental killing. Whenever the thought that David might have spun them a tall tale that night crossed his mind, he thrust it from him. Sure, that was a weakling's way, but for a long time now he hadn't kidded himself that he was anything else.

Beside him, Consuelo Bryant and Doris were discussing Gimbel's new store on Eighty-sixth Street. As always when those two talked to each other, their voices held a hostile edge. The new store, Doris complained, was "bringing mobs of people to the neighborhood," to which Consuelo answered, "Well, not being a Mrs. Gotrocks, I can't afford to be sensitive about crowds. I'm damned glad to have a department store within walking distance."

On the other side of him, May Cosgrove was talking about Krishnamurti to Henry Maize, who listened with his usual patient courtesy. As he often did, George wondered just what David had on Henry Maize. Perhaps that time three summers ago when David had hitched a ride with Henry up to Massachusetts, the older man had gotten into some godawful mess. Something including a woman, perhaps. That could happen to a man like Henry, a widower, lonely.

Standing a little apart from the others, David and Paul were talking about a song, evidently one they'd collaborated on. George heard Paul say, "Now that you've touched it up here and there, I think I may have a hit on my hands. Of course, I'm counting on you to get it a hearing."

"Don't worry about that," David answered. "I'll take it down to Carson and Hapgood Monday morning."

Hearing the false enthusiasm in the younger man's voice, George thought with grim amusement, "Everything has its price, David my boy."

Doris, he noticed, had turned away from Consuelo, and was also listening to David and Paul. Her gaze, resting on David's profile, was so nakedly enamored that George felt, not jealousy—that had died many years ago—but a twinge of embarrassment.

David, George reflected, probably felt more sure of Doris's silence than of Paul's, say. But he might be in for a little surprise there. George knew that Doris could get over a crush, even a long-standing one, with the suddenness of a high-school girl turning from one "steady" boy friend to a new one.

It was funny how little age seemed to have to do with maturity. His wife often reminded him of a teen-ager. On the other hand the little Wentworth girl, half Doris's age, seemed thoroughly grown up.

What, he wondered, had happened between Karen and David after he hurried down the hill in pursuit of her the evening before? Whatever it was, apparently it was keeping her away. If she intended to appear on the hill tonight, undoubtedly she'd have done so by now.

Again he thought, "She's lucky to be clear of this." He just hoped she'd stay clear.

The quiet throb of an engine. Turning, he saw one of the park's motor scooters, driven by a blue-helmeted policeman, move along the broad asphalt walk which paralleled the museum's west wall. As always when he saw a scooter on the walk, or a prowl car on the road about twenty yards beyond the walk, he felt a momentary fear that the vehicle would stop and a uniformed figure would stride toward the group. It was an absurd fear, he knew. If the police became interested in them again, they'd be questioned separately and by detectives, just as they'd been the day after Herman Dock-weiler's death. But George suspected that the others shared that irrational fear. He'd noticed that they all fell silent whenever a motor scooter drew near.

The policeman glanced at them casually as his scooter carried him slowly past. Then, following the curved path, he turned the nose of his vehicle toward the distant towers of the apartment houses on Central Park West.

Well, for still one more night they'd presented a picture of normality to the gaze of the law—just a group of eastside dog owners, meeting at their accustomed spot on the hill. And now that they had, George hoped that Doris would want to go home.

"Let's go," he said. "It's too damned cold up here."

"If you'd wear ski boots like David, instead of those silly old-fashioned galoshes—" But she snapped her fingers to Henri and patted the woolly brown head while George fastened the leash. Around them the others were calling their dogs. With the poodle struggling ahead of them through the snow, Doris and George descended the hill.

May Cosgrove touched David's arm. "Could you walk part of the way home with me? There's something I have to tell you."

Feeling an unpleasant premonition, he smiled down at the serene face, with its halo of white curls topped by an ancient black plush pillbox. "Why, of course." Turning to the others, he said, "Don't wait for us. Mrs. Cosgrove and I have something to talk over."

Hand under her elbow, he shepherded May Cosgrove and her Sistie and the Great Dane down the hill. By the time they reached the sidewalk running along the museum's north wall, none of the others were in sight. "Now," he asked, "what's the trouble?"

"No trouble, David dear. It's just that Karen Wentworth came to see me this afternoon."

That unpleasant premonition grew sharper. "Yes?"

"I told her about your—accident. That poor Mr. Dock-weiler, I mean."

He stopped short. Something seemed to explode in his head. "You idiot," he wanted to scream at her, "you bloody old lunatic." For a moment, fighting for control, he said nothing. Then he asked, "Why did you do that?"

"It seemed the best thing to do. Don't look so troubled, dear. Don't you see? She'll help protect you. She loves you very much, David."

He thought, "Not anymore." Pain and a sense of loss mingling with his fear, he remembered the terrified repulsion in her hazel eyes as she lay there on the subway platform.

"Come on, David. Let's keep walking."

Mechanically, he obeyed. "What did she say she was going to do about it?"

Trying to remember the girl's exact words, May Cosgrove said, "Well, she didn't say anything definite. But I know it's all right. She was *meant* to know, David. Suddenly it came to me that she was. Otherwise the two things I'd done to make her stay away from you and from the hill would have worked. But the very first night after I'd sent the telegram, she came up there—"

"So it was you who had her dog picked up." Somehow, he was able to smile down at her. "I thought it was."

"Yes. And then there was the marzipan. That didn't work either."

"The marzipan?"

As they moved north on Fifth Avenue, past doormen peering out through snugly closed glass doors, she told him about the marzipan.

He asked in a thick voice, "Does she know you sent it?"

"No, I felt it wasn't necessary to tell her I had. I mean, the candy isn't important now."

He felt an almost irresistible desire to put his hands around her neck and squeeze. God! What had she done to him? Poisoned candy! Why, after that business in the subway, Karen must feel sure he'd sent it. And there went his last chance that she'd keep quiet about Herman Dockweiler.

He asked, "Did she mention suspecting anyone? Me, for instance?"

"You!" May Cosgrove's tone was astounded. "Of course not, dear. I do think, though, that she'd gone to the shop to try to find out who'd bought the candy. She had a box of their chocolate creams with her when she called on me."

His anxiety lessened a little. If she'd given his description to the shop people, then she must be fairly sure now that he hadn't bought the candy.

"You know the shop I mean, David. It's half a block from my place."

"Yes, I know." Again with that sense of loss, he remembered how lighthearted he'd felt as he ordered that box of candy for Karen last Christmas. Could that be only about a month and a half ago? It felt like two years.

"What did she say she was going to do with the candy?"

"I think she'll dispose of it. In the bathroom," May said delicately. "That's what I advised her to do."

Oh, no, she wouldn't. She'd turn it over to the police for analysis. And the police, because of that subway business, would question him. What was worse, some bright boy on the force would remember that a David Bryant had also been questioned about the death of that old bookseller. . . .

Get that candy. Since she hadn't turned it over to the police by the time she called on May Cosgrove, probably she didn't intend to do so until tomorrow.

He asked, "Did she say where she was keeping the candy?"

"Locked in her desk. Her dog, you know. He's very fond of sweets."

Maybe all wasn't lost. Maybe nothing was lost. If she'd see him, if she'd let him into her apartment, maybe he could persuade her to keep quiet about what this dotty May Cosgrove had told her. Part of her, he knew, must want to keep quiet about it. If she hadn't retained some tenderness for him, surely she'd have made a charge against him last night. All he had to do was to supply her with reasons, ones her conscience could accept, for keeping quiet.

He began to marshal arguments. It had been an accident. The old man was mortally ill anyway. Most important of all, he, David, by keeping silent this long—a silence he'd admit had been cowardly and foolish—had probably let himself in for a much longer prison sentence than he would otherwise have received.

That would be his argument. A number of years in prison, and the wrecking of his whole career, against the life of a man who'd have died anyway within a few months.

As for the candy, once he was in her apartment, he'd manage to get hold of it. Probably she'd left the desk key right in the lock. He'd suggest that she make coffee, for instance, and while she was in the kitchen . . .

But what if she wasn't at home tonight? There was that damned Bill Bailey. She'd sounded quite taken with him. He had a sudden vision of her at some restaurant table, telling all she'd learned from Mrs. Cosgrove to the man opposite her. No! Don't think about it. He'd find her at home. And even if he didn't, he thought grimly, he'd get in someway, and remove that poisoned candy. That fire escape outside her window. She'd told him that her landlady had talked of installing bars at that window, but David knew she hadn't done so before Karen went down to Raleigh, and probably she hadn't gotten around to it since. What's more, Karen was a fresh-air fiend. When he'd come to her apartment in even the chilliest December weather, he'd noticed that her window was open a few inches. The only problem would be the screen.

And the dog. But Bozo knew him, and so there'd be no big problem there.

Lexington Avenue just ahead. He waited until they reached the corner, and then halted. "Mrs. Cosgrove, would you mind doing me a favor?"

The gentle old face looked up at him. "Of course not, dear."

He took out his wallet. "That candy shop will still be open, since it's a weekend night. Would you buy some marzipan for me? I want to send it to an aunt of mine. I'd buy it myself, but I'm expecting an important phone call. I'll nip over to my apartment, and then come to your place to pick up the candy."

Mrs. Cosgrove looked at the five-dollar bill he'd given her. "How much marzipan, David?"

"Oh, I don't know. How much did you buy this morning? A pound?" She nodded. "Well, make it a pound." He decided to essay a small joke. "But no roach poison, please. I like my aunt."

"Oh, David!" The surprisingly young blue eyes behind the glasses were reproachful. "Of course not. I did that only to protect *you*. I was wrong, of course, as I later realized, but—"

"I know, dear. I was only joking. Well, nip on down to the shop before it closes."

"But five dollars is much too much."

"You can give me the change when I pick up the candy, about twenty minutes from now."

"And you'll have some supper? I always have mine before I take Sistie up to the hill, but I know you don't. And I could join you for a bite or two. I'll make some lovely creamed tuna."

Creamed tuna. Well, it couldn't be helped. "Sounds great. See you in a few minutes," he said, and turned away.

14

The lobby of the Gloria Arms Apartment Hotel on West Forty-seventh Street—Rooms by Day, Week, or Month—was not much larger than the average living room. The globes in two parchment reading lamps flanking a sofa of cracked black plastic were so thriftily dim that one could have read by them only at peril of going blind. The air held a mingled smell of insecticide, stale tobacco smoke, and something else that Karen couldn't define. Stale lives, perhaps.

At the rear of the lobby, a long-faced man of about fifty, bald head shining beneath a green-shaded droplight, stood behind a semicircular desk. As Karen approached him, she was nervously conscious of his flat, unwinking stare.

"Miss Wentworth to see Mr. Thompson. I'm expected," she added firmly.

"I know. He phoned down." While he stared at her for another long moment, she could read the puzzled surprise in his pale blue eyes—eyes that probably were seldom surprised at anything.

"Elevator's over there," he said finally. "Room 502."

The small automatic elevator, its air smelling even more strongly of stale tobacco smoke, seemed to be afflicted with palsy. When it came to a shuddering stop, the door slid back. Over carpet so frayed that its pattern was undistinguishable, she moved down a feebly lit corridor until she found a door labeled, in flaking gilt paint, 502.

For several uneasy moments she stood motionless. She was beginning to regret the impulse that had led her to make an appointment with a perhaps unsavory stranger in a Times Square hotel. But over the phone Slide Thompson's voice, with its nasal southwestern tones, hadn't sounded like a drug addict's. He'd sounded harmless and pleasant, so much so that a plausible excuse for seeking an interview had popped into her head.

Well, if she didn't like his looks when he opened the door, she'd just turn and walk rapidly toward that staircase landing at the end of the corridor.

She knocked. She heard a chair scrape over a floor. Then the door opened.

He appeared harmless and pleasant, too—a small, wiry man not much larger than a jockey, with straight brown hair that looked freshly slicked back. He'd dressed neatly if rather gaudily in a tan suit with a fine-lined red check and a paisley tie. His face, like that of so many jazz musicians, had remained amazingly young. Except for the bags under his brown eyes, he might have been still in his thirties.

"Miss Wentworth?" Karen caught a whiff of Bourbon.

"That's right."

"Come in, come in."

It was a sad little room. A sagging studio couch. One straight chair, and one armchair, upholstered in frayed green plush. A new but cheap-looking bureau of varnished knotty pine, with toilet articles neatly arrayed on its top. Against one wall, near a curtained alcove that probably concealed a gas plate and a sink, stood a trombone's long black case.

He waved his hand at the armchair. "Sit down, Miss Wentworth; sit down." He crossed the room to a flimsy table that held a quart bottle, two thick tumblers, and a water pitcher. Lifting the bottle, he asked, "Do you indulge?"

"Sometimes. But I'd rather not now, thanks."

"Mind if I do?"

"Not at all."

She watched him pour about an inch of brown liquid into one of the tumblers. A drug addict? She was no expert in such matters, but she'd heard that people on narcotics had little taste for alcohol.

After adding water to the glass, he carried it over to the studio couch and sat down. "No ice, you notice? People say that's English, not liking ice in your drinks, but I was never in England in my life." He paused. "What college you say you go to? NYU?"

She nodded. "I'm a graduate student."

"And you want to do a theme for a course you're taking? A theme about guys like me?" He looked pleased, but puzzled.

"That's right." After a moment she added, "The course is called, 'Aspects of Popular Culture.' "

He shook his head wonderingly. "The things they think up these days." Then, with a wry glance at the trombone case: "Well, I don't know whether I belong in a theme about popular anything. Only a few of the old-time Dixieland musicians work steady these days, and I'm not one of them. What I mean is, Miss Wentworth, why me? If you wanted to talk to a slide man who's still up there, why didn't you phone Muff Morton? He's in town, working at the Riverboat."

"I called you because a friend of mine mentioned you." She paused, hearbeats quickening, eyes fixed on the little man's face. "His name's David Bryant."

He said in an astonished tone, "David Bryant!"

"Don't you know him?"

"I know who he is." Thompson's voice held respect tinged with envy. "But his gig's real different from mine. Modern stuff. Besides, he's a lot younger than me, and pretty successful and all. I'm surprised he even remembered my name. I only met him a couple of times."

"When did you first meet him?"

"Oh, about a year ago. I was filling in for another trombonist, a pal of mine, on one of the TV talk shows. David Bryant was being interviewed on the show." Embarrassment crossed his face. "As a matter of fact—maybe he told you—I hit him up for a ten-spot that night. A horse I been depending on had run out of the money, and this David Bryant and I got to talking after the show, and he seemed such a nice young guy—well, I put the arm on him."

With a smile that she hoped would take any possible offense out of the question, she asked lightly, "Ever pay it back?"

"As a matter of fact, I did. Ran into him on the street one day, oh, about a month ago. I was pretty flush that day flush for me, anyway—so I handed him the ten-spot. He looked real surprised. Guess he'd forgotten about loaning it to me."

About a month ago. Perhaps on the same date that an elderly bookstore owner had fallen in the snow-curtained darkness of Central Park. . . .

"What do you want me to talk about, Miss Wentworth?" She took a black notebook and a green ballpoint pen from her shoulder bag. "Well, you must have known a lot of famous musicians."

"I sure have. When I was just a kid, fifteen or so, Bix Biederbicke let me sit in with him."

Pausing now and then to drink from the tumbler, he went on talking. Great names rolled off his tongue. Fats Waller, Jack Teagarden, Sidney Bechet. He spoke of famous places, too. New Orleans' Bourbon Street, and Beale Street in Memphis, and New York's Fifty-second Street after the Second World War. Karen knew enough about the origins of jazz to realize, feeling amused and touched, that he was cleaning up its history for her. The establishments in which Jelly

113

Roll Morton perfected his brilliant piano style became "night clubs," and the ladies employed there "hostesses, sort of."

Finally she glanced at her watch. Almost nine-thirty. Closing the notebook, she said, "Thank you very much, Mr. Thompson. You've given me a lot of material."

"A pleasure." He eyed her wistfully. "If you find you need more information, I'd be glad to oblige you, anytime."

"If I do, I'll certainly call you."

He moved with her across the room. At the door, she turned. "Oh, there's something I almost forgot. I'm not sure, but it seems to me that David Bryant said something about meeting you in the park one night last January. In that playing field about two hundred yards west of the museum."

The astonishment in his face appeared completely genuine. "Me? In Central Park at night? Unless I had a squad of musclemen along," he said fervently, "I wouldn't go two hundred yards into Central Park at night for a thousand dollars."

15

David had been unable to escape May Cosgrove and her creamed tuna and her chatter until almost nine. Now, his heartbeats rapid with annoyance and anxiety, he walked swiftly to Karen's apartment house.

In the foyer, he placed a gloved forefinger on the push button beside her name, waited a moment, rang again. When she didn't answer, he looked at the closed front door. This morning, May Cosgrove had said, she'd found the door standing ajar. But no such luck for him. He tried the knob. Yes, locked.

Turning back to the panel that held the push buttons and the intercom grille, he scanned the rows of names and then pushed the bell labeled "G. L. Trent." Almost immediately the grille made a squawking noise. "Yes?" a man's voice asked suspiciously. "Who is it?" Not answering, David rang the bell of a Mr. and Mrs. Schroeder in apartment 5-D. The Schroeders were either trusting souls or expecting a visitor, because after two or three seconds he heard the buzzing mechanism which released the latch. Lunging at the door, he went inside and then moved rapidly and quietly down the lower hall to a door labeled "Basement and Laundry."

Its knob turned under his hand. He descended steps to a cement-floored room. Overhead, among a maze of steam-pipes, a caged light bulb shone down on a washing machine, a dryer, and a number of trunks and storage boxes.

Quickly he moved toward a metal door, secured by a heavy bolt in the far wall. If there was a lock, too . . . But there wasn't. The knob turned easily. He pulled the bolt back and, closing the door soundlessly after him, stepped out into a cement-floored rear court, surrounded on three sides by a high wooden fence. Light filtering from windows in Karen's building, as well as from back windows of the building beyond the fence, showed him the fire escape that ran past Karen's window.

He stood there for a moment, listening to the jumbled murmur of half a dozen TV sets, and then turned toward the fire escape. As he climbed, he was uneasily aware of the half-dozen or so darkened windows beyond the fence. At any one of those windows someone might be standing, someone who in another moment might turn to the phone and call the police. But better to risk that, he thought grimly, than to let that box of poisoned candy remain in Karen's desk.

Approaching that third-floor window, he slowed his pace. There was just a chance that she was at home, after all. Nervously and physically exhausted, she might have decided to ignore the telephone and doorbell. Perhaps she lay in the dark now, trying to make up her mind what to do about him. . . .

He crouched at the sill. Light shining from beneath a window shade opposite showed him that her own windowpane was raised a few inches. His only problem would be the screen.

For perhaps a minute he remained motionless, listening. Not a sound from inside the room. He reached into a jacket pocket for the gold-plated penknife. The knife, an expensive gadget from Tiffany's, was one of the two articles for which he'd returned to his apartment earlier that evening, after sending May Cosgrove to the candy shop. Two years earlier a girl had given it to him for his birthday. At the time, with no idea of how much he was going to need it, he'd considered it a silly sort of gift. Even though he'd worn his lightest gloves, his fingers felt a little awkward as he inserted the knife at the right lower corner of the screen's frame and began to cut through the worn mesh.

Inside the room, coming suddenly awake, Bozo exploded into furious barking. Even though he'd been prepared for that, David felt an almost painful leap of his heart. "Quiet, Bozo," he said softly. "You know me."

Bozo's barking subsided to uneasy whines. He recognized the voice. But what was its owner doing out there beyond the window? And why was the man afraid? Bozo could smell his fear.

David, deciding it was less risky to make noise than to remain out there on the fire escape any longer than necessary, ripped the knife along the entire lower edge of the half-rotten screen, and an inch or so up the side. Reaching in, he unfastened the hook, swung the screen out, and pushed the window sash upward. He stepped over the sill.

Again Bozo barked. Obviously, though, he hadn't yet decided to attack. David could see the dim shape of the dog backing away toward the far wall. He lowered the window shade. Then, moving confidently across the small room to the switch beside the door, he turned on the overhead light. Bozo, the very picture of ambivalence—plumy tail wagging, but eyes uneasy and suspicious—watched David as he walked over to the desk.

Damn! The key wasn't in the lock. Probably she had it with her. He'd have to jimmy the lock, and if he damaged it, or made a scratch on the rosewood, she'd know that someone . . .

Turning, he looked around the room. His eyes found the little blue jar atop the bookcase. To women, he'd observed, such objects were more than ornaments or containers for flowers. They dropped almost everything into them—souvenir matchbooks, broken earrings, keys . . .

Walking over to the bookcase, he turned the jar upside-down. The little brass key fell into his palm. Recrossing the room, he opened the desk drawer. There it all was, the wrapping paper, the coil of silver ribbon, the card addressed to Miss Karen Wentworth, and the candy box.

Even though he doubted she'd notice any change, he studied for a moment the arrangement of the box and its wrappings. Then he picked up the little envelope and took out the card.

Damn that dotty Cosgrove woman! "Hoping for forgiveness." After that business in the subway, such a message could have had only one meaning for Karen. Why, his name might as well have been signed to it. Thank God Karen had thought of going around to the sweetshop where, hopefully, she'd become convinced that he hadn't been a customer today.

With angry swiftness, he laid the envelope on the desk and stuffed wrapping paper, ribbon, and finally the candy box into one pocket of his duffel coat. Then very carefully, so as not to tear the paper, he took from his other coat pocket the identically wrapped package May Cosgrove had bought for him.

The downstairs buzzer gave two sharp rings.

He froze. The dog, again catching the scent of fear, made a sound that was more growl than whine.

After a moment David relaxed. His first panicky thought had been that Karen, returning, had discovered she didn't have her front door key. But in that case, of course, she'd have rung the landlady's bell, not this one.

Again the buzzer sounded. Whoever was down there was hopping mad. Karen's would-be visitor had jabbed a finger against the button and held it there.

After about a minute the buzzing ceased. With Bozo, quiet now, sniffing at his heels, he went into the kitchen and turned on the light. Laying the box on the enamel-topped table, he took off the lid, and then reached into the inside breast pocket of his jacket for the second of the articles he'd brought from his apartment, an old-fashioned stickpin which had been among the miscellaneous objects in the trunk shipped to him after his father's death. Taking out one of the little marzipan apples, he lifted it from its paper cup, made a tiny hole in its underside with the point of the stickpin, and laid it, restored to its cup, on the table.

Beside him, Bozo made a begging whine. "Sorry, chum," David said.

Ten minutes later he stared at the candies strewn over the table, each in its paper cup, each bearing a small puncture. Should he restore them to the box in their original order? Reaching into his pocket, he brought out the box containing May Cosgrove's lethal goodies, took off the lid, and saw that Karen had replaced them at random, not bothering to make separate rows of the tiny pumpkins, apples, and bananas. Working swiftly now, he refilled the other box in the same careless fashion and, after turning off the light, carried the box and its wrapping back to the living room. He placed the paper, ribbon, and box in the drawer, and laid the little envelope containing May Cosgrove's message atop the box. Crossing the room, he restored the desk key to the blue jar.

Before he switched off the light, he said, "Good night, Bozo."

Pushing the screen's frame outward, he stepped onto the fire escape. When he'd lowered the sash to its former position, he eased the window screen back into place, reached in through the gap in the mesh, and refastened the hook. Last of all, he pulled the severed edge of the screening outward and then smoothed it back into place. With luck, several days might pass before Karen noticed the cut.

Quickly and noiselessly, he descended the fire escape. Re-entering the basement, he bolted the door, ascended steps, and cautiously opened the door onto the first-floor hallway. It was empty. He walked out into the night.

16

Leaving Slide Thompson's frowzy hotel, Karen turned onto Broadway. As she walked toward the Forty-second Street subway stop, she was only dimly aware of garish posters outside movie grind houses, and penny arcades spilling glare and the crack of rifles, and a passing man who said, "Hello, honey." Descending littered steps, she took the shuttle train which connected with the eastside subway. Throughout the brief ride, she stared unseeingly at a soft drink ad above the heads of the passengers opposite her.

Had Thompson told her the truth? One of his statements, about the ten-dollar loan, confirmed the story David had told May Cosgrove and the others. But that wasn't the vital point. What mattered was whether or not Thompson had arranged to meet David in the park that night. And Thompson had denied, with vigor, that he'd even contemplated such a meeting.

She'd found herself liking the little man. But that proved nothing. He could still be everything that David had said he was. Karen could have no illusion that she possessed an infallible ability to read human nature. After all, she thought wretchedly, she'd loved David and hoped to spend the rest of her life with him. And even at the most charitable estimate, David was a man too weak and cowardly to report his accidental slaying of another human being.

She needed to know more about the old man who'd died that night. Perhaps then this fog of doubt and indecision clouding her vision would thin a little. She wouldn't wait until Bill's policeman friend found time to go through the official files on recent homicides. After all, she could do the job more quickly than Detective Rossi, because now she knew which particular case of homicide to focus her attention upon, and neither the police nor Bill knew that. Tomorrow morning she'd go down to the *Times* and look through microfilmed back issues for the story of Herman Dockweiler's death.

The shuttle came to a jerky halt. Getting out, she walked beneath the guiding row of light bulbs in the tunnel ceiling toward the uptown train.

She had to wait for it a long time. Her watch said five after ten by the time she came above ground at the Eighty-sixth Street stop. She hurried east and then south toward her apartment house.

She was only a yard or so from her front steps when the door of a white station wagon parked at the curb swung back. A tall man got out and seized her arm. "Where the hell have you been?"

She gave a smothered scream. Then she saw that it was Bill's face scowling down at her. "Bill! You scared me."

"Scared you! What do you think you've been doing to me? You don't even wait to talk to me on the phone. You just leave a message saying you can't see me. I tried to phone you, and when that didn't work, I came over here and rang your bell. The first time was around seven-thirty. I came back again around nine, and when there was still no answer, I decided to drive over here and wait."

Glancing past him, she saw that on the station wagon's front door, painted in black letters, were the words "Bill Bailey's Kennels." She said, "I'm sorry, but I don't see why you're so upset."

"Upset! You nearly get killed by a subway train. Some-

121

body leaves candy for you that might be poisoned. And then you just disappear for an evening. How the hell do you expect me to feel?"

"Don't swear so much."

"I'll swear all I want to. Now answer my question."

A passing woman threw them an amused glance. "Domestic fight," Karen could imagine the woman thinking. And no wonder. That was exactly how Bill sounded—like a suspicious, outraged husband.

"Where have you been?" he repeated.

Mutely she looked up at him. She couldn't tell him. For one thing, if he learned that she'd spent an hour in a fleabag hotel with a strange and perhaps dangerous man, Bill in his present mood might explode into little pieces, right there on the sidewalk. For another, she couldn't explain about Slide Thompson without telling what she'd learned from May Cosgrove. And she wasn't ready to divulge that to anyone—not yet.

"I went to see a married friend of mine. She's just broken up with her husband, and she was feeling very low and wanted to talk to me."

He studied her face. "You're a little liar."

She said, with a resentment only sharpened by her guilt, "If that's the way you feel about me—" and turned toward the apartment house steps.

He caught her arm. "All right, all right! Maybe you're not a liar. Anyway, let's get that candy so Frank Rossi can have it analyzed."

They climbed two flights of stairs to her apartment door. On the other side of it, Bozo whined eagerly. She unlocked the door, patted the dog's ecstatically wriggling back, and then touched the light switch. "Come in, Bill."

While he stood in the center of the room, she took the little brass key from the blue jar and unlocked the desk drawer. "Here it is."

Crossing to her side, he looked into the drawer for a moment. "Mind if I use this newspaper?"

"Of course not."

Bending, he drew that morning's *Times* from the magazine rack beside the desk. He opened the newspaper out on the carpet and then, handling the objects as gingerly as possible, laid the box and its wrappings and the card on the outspread paper. "Prints," he explained, carefully folding the edges of the newspaper over. "Of course, if the candy's okay, there'll be no need to test for fingerprints."

He stood up. "Well," he said, tucking the newspaper-wrapped parcel under his arm, "I'll take this down to Frank first thing in the morning. And I'll ask him to get cracking on those files of recent homicides.

After a moment she said, "No."

"What do you mean, no?"

"I'd like to have the candy analyzed, but as for the rest, I just want to drop it."

"Drop it! This Bryant tries to kill you in the subway—"

"We don't know that he did."

"And we don't know that he didn't. And if he did, maybe it was because he thought you might find out about something else he'd done."

She said desperately, "I'm never going to see David again. Isn't that enough? Let's just drop the whole thing."

"If the guy's in the clear, what harm could we do him? And if he isn't, we ought to know about it. Everybody ought to. So why do you ask me to drop it?"

"Because I loved David!" she wanted to cry out. "It must be awful to see a man you once loved arrested, and doubly awful when it's through you that he was caught. If I'm to turn him in, I want it to be by my own decision, and in my own time."

She said aloud, "Bill, I'm grateful to you. But after all, this isn't really any of your business."

Color spread slowly over his face. "It's funny, but I'd begun to feel that anything that concerned you was my business. Well, good night." He turned toward the door. "And incidentally, to hell with you, too."

As she watched him with miserable eyes, he put his hand on the doorknob, hesitated, and then swung around. "I didn't mean that."

He crossed to where she stood. Hand under her chin, he tilted her face up and kissed her. "I don't think I could ever mean it," he said.

Her smile was shaky. "I'm awfully glad to hear that."

"And I can see why you want to forget about the whole thing," he went on. "All of this must be a great strain on you. I'll have the candy analyzed right way. But as for the rest of it, we won't even talk about it until later on."

Karen found something wonderfully warm and comforting about those last two words. "Yes," she said, "later on."

17

Although it was past her bedtime, May Cosgrove sat wide awake in her rocking chair. In the past hour, just the tiniest little doubt had crept into her thoughts. Perhaps her first instinct about the girl had been the correct one. Perhaps it had been a mistake to take Karen into her confidence. Certainly David had thought so. He'd tried to hide it, dear boy that he was, but he'd been very upset, so much so that he hadn't seemed able to really enjoy their little supper together.

Well, if she had made an error, she could rectify it. Inspiration would come to her. It always did.

She began to rock vigorously.

In the living room of his penthouse apartment, George Kinsing had just made a discovery. He didn't like his dog. With that ruff around his neck and that blue bow Doris tied on top of his head, Henri didn't even look like a dog.

Before they went to Italy—and they'd better go soon, because George felt that any day now *he* might land in that Connecticut sanitarium—before they went to Italy, he'd try to persuade Doris to give the poodle away.

Italy. If only nothing came up to prevent their going. Nothing better had, he thought grimly.

Across the room, seated before the TV set, his wife stared

at Englebert Humperdinck, and thought of Karen Wentworth. Doris had felt sick, actually sick, when David chased down the hill after the girl last evening. But apparently he'd done so only to get rid of her once and for all, because she'd stayed away from their group on the hill this evening. Whatever he'd said or done to her served her right for trying to cling to him when it was obvious he'd come to prefer women who were—well, more mature. What was more, she could make trouble for David, for all of them.

But if she did, Doris vowed silently, she was certainly going to wish she hadn't.

Henry Maize, in pajamas and dressing gown, helped the aged cocker spaniel onto Myra's bed. Myra, he knew, wouldn't have minded. When his wife was alive, Fluff had often slept on the foot of her bed.

Sitting down on the edge of his own bed, Henry resumed his conversation with his dead wife. It was a conversation he carried on at intervals almost every day of his life, while riding the subway, for instance, or drawing a drink from the office water cooler. But it was only in the bedroom that he spoke to her aloud.

"The point is, Myra," he said, "that I haven't acted this way to save my own skin. It's been for our son, and the grandchildren. They don't deserve to be disgraced by me. Now that I'm in this deep, I'd do almost anything to save them disgrace. You understand that, don't you, Myra? They're your grandchildren, too."

In the living room of the apartment he shared with two other men—one a waiter at a Longchamps restaurant, the other a theater box-office man—Paul Winship sat at his upright piano. For two hours he'd been playing his own songs. That was the nice part about having roommates who worked at night. You could play the piano almost as late as you wanted to.

Squinting through the smoke of his cigarette, he placed on the piano rack one of the songs that he and David had gone over a few nights before. He laid the cigarette in a tray beside him on the piano bench and played the song through.

It was good, he decided. It was damned good, now that David had touched it up a little here and there.

David. An ugly expression crossed Paul's face. He could tell David didn't think he had any talent. David was wrong. He had plenty of talent. It was just that he'd never got the hang of those little tricks of composition that could make the difference between a flop and a hit.

Well, David knew those tricks, and David had connections with music publishers, and he was going to use them both for the benefit of his old pal Paul Winship for a long, long time.

Maybe David thought that when he finally skipped out for Paris or Marrakesh or someplace, he'd be free of the people he'd persuaded to cover up for him. Well, David had a surprise in store. Wherever he went, he'd be apt to find a Paul Winship song in his morning mail. And if he was smart, he'd tinker with all those songs, and pull whatever strings he could to get them published. Probably after a while Paul wouldn't need David. He himself would have learned all the tricks and made the connections. But for as long as he did need David . . .

After all, there was no statute of limitations on murder.

The future looked great. People pointing him out. "There's Paul Winship. He's up for an Oscar this year." A big apartment, where he'd live alone or with someone really compatible, not with Darrel and Bruce, who were always teaming up to complain about something—his playing the piano on weekends, or not getting his share of the rent up on time. He'd drive a Ferrari, and buy all his clothes at Brooks'. No, he'd have them made in London.

Stand aside, Burt Bacharach, here I come.

If only someone didn't blow the whistle on David.

That Wentworth girl. He'd had an uneasy feeling ever since, last Monday night, he'd seen that mutt of hers charging up the hill. And the fact that she hadn't shown up this evening didn't really ease his mind. He'd been able to tell even last Monday that the girl sensed something had happened while she was away. And then some idiot had arranged for her dog to be taken . . .

May Cosgrove. He was sure she'd pulled that stunt, although when he'd asked her about it, she'd smiled and said, "Now why would I do a thing like that?"

Well, no matter what the girl suspected, she'd damn well better keep her suspicions to herself.

With a force that bent the cylinder and split the white paper, he rubbed out the cigarette in the ashtray beside him.

In her apartment above her photographic studio, Consuelo Bryant lay asleep and dreaming. In the dream she stood in her darkroom downstairs, developing a photograph whose subject she couldn't make out. David walked in and turned on the light.

"Something terrible has happened," he said. "There's an epidemic of a new disease. It kills women."

Her dreaming self felt a leap of terror.

"Don't be afraid," David said. "It kills only women under thirty. Karen caught it. She's dead."

"Oh, David! I'm so sorry."

But even in the dream she knew she was glad.

18

Around ten the next morning, Karen was awakened by the ringing of the telephone on the little stand beside her studio bed. Groggily, she reached out for the instrument. "Hello."

Bill's voice asked, "Did I wake you?"

"That's all right. I should have been up long ago." She threw a guilty glance at Bozo. Patiently awaiting his long overdue breakfast and his usual Saturday morning walk around the neighborhood, he lay with muzzle sunk on his outstretched paws.

"Well, I just heard from Frank Rossi. That candy is clean as a whistle. Nothing in it but sugar, almond paste, and the other usual ingredients."

"Oh, I'm so glad!" In her half-awakened state, she thought for one confused but wonderful moment that her dilemma had disappeared. Then she realized that of course it hadn't. It was good to hear that neither David nor anyone else had tried to poison her. But that didn't alter the ugly fact of Herman Dockweiler's death.

Bill said, "How about making up for that date you broke with me? Dinner tonight?"

Before evening, there'd be plenty of time to look up the newspaper accounts of the Dockweiler case. "I'd love it."

"Around seven-thirty all right?"

"Fine."

For a long moment, while he hesitated, she feared he was going to suggest again that he have his detective friend look up the police files on recent homicides. But all he said was "See you then," and hung up.

After she'd showered and dressed, fed Bozo and herself, and taken him over to Carl Schurz Park and back, she set about her usual weekend tasks. Doing her fingernails. Mending a bra strap. Washing underthings and stockings. Even as she swirled soap chips around in the wash basin, she knew that she was stalling. Except for her manicure, all these tasks could have waited until the next day. The truth was that she really didn't want to know what the *Times* had written about the old man found dead in the park. Perhaps it was partly the threatening grayness outside and the increasing heaviness of the atmosphere as the barometer fell, but she was aware of a growing sense of dread. "Just leave it alone," a voice within her kept saying. "Leave it *alone*." But of course she couldn't.

The coming snowfall was a big one, her radio warned. It might last as long as twelve hours. The mayor himself came on the air. With his voice holding wry recollection of a former snowfall that had cost him thousands of votes in Queens, he assured his constituents that snow-removal equipment was standing by "in all boroughs."

Around two, as she was descending the stairs with Bozo beside her, it suddenly came to her that perhaps she should go back to the apartment and exchange her shoulder bag, with its damaged strap, for another one. *No,* she told herself. No more stalling.

She left Bozo with Mrs. Orford—a shopping trip, she explained—and set out for the subway stop. Grayish rather than white in the afternoon light, snow was already falling. It came straight down through the windless air, in small dry flakes of the sort that soon begin to accumulate rather than melt on contact with cement or bare earth. By the time she came aboveground at Times Square, street lamps and shop window lights had been turned on, sending a wan glow through the curtain of snowflakes.

Perhaps because of the storm, the *Times* reading room was almost empty. Walking up to a severe-faced woman who sat behind a long counter, Karen said, "I'd like to look up some back issues of the *Times.*"

Without speaking, the woman tore the top sheet of a pad of small printed forms and laid it on the counter. Karen studied the form. It held spaces for her name, address, dates of the back copies she wanted to see, and her reason for wanting to see them.

It would have to be the same reason she'd given Slide Thompson. She picked up a yellow pencil stub attached to a short chain and filled in the form. In the last space she wrote, "Research for theme, *Asp'ts Pop. Cult.,* NYU." Would the woman ask for some proof that she was enrolled at NYU?

To her surprise, the woman glanced at the slip, ripped it in two, and dropped the pieces into some receptacle invisible to Karen behind the counter. "You don't need that," she snapped. "Recent copies are over there. You walked right by them."

Feeling relieved, Karen murmured an apology and moved to a long reading stand, its top set at an angle for comfortable perusal of the large volumes resting on it. She found the volume which held the early January issues, and turned to the paper for the eleventh, the day after Herman Dockweiler had died. May Cosgrove had said that the *Times* didn't carry the story that morning, but she might have been wrong about that.

Mrs. Cosgrove hadn't been wrong. Karen turned to the index of the issue for January twelfth. Under "Other News," she found the listing for "Bookseller Found Shot to Death in Central Park." In all probability the *Daily News* had bannerlined the story. But the good gray *Times,* with characteristic distaste for violent death, had printed the story on page three. With fingers that were somewhat unsteady, she turned back the front page of the paper's first section.

In general, the newspaper account of the body's discovery corroborated what May Cosgrove had told her. About eight o'clock on the morning of January eleventh, a sanitation worker assigned to Central Park had stumbled across a body, completely covered by the previous night's snowfall, in one of the park's playing fields. The dead man, later identified as Herman Dockweiler, aged sixty-nine, had been shot three times through the heart with bullets from a twenty-two caliber pistol. The weapon hadn't been found. Snow had obliterated any footprints that otherwise might have been discovered. Because of the body's half-frozen condition, the medical examiner had been unable to fix the time of death any more closely than sometime between six P.M. and midnight. For the present, police had ruled out robbery as a motive, since the victim's wallet, pocket watch, and wide gold wedding ring were all found on the body.

Mr. Dockweiler and his wife, Irma, had come from Melbourne, Australia, to New York shortly before World War Two. For the past thirty years they'd operated a small shop, Dockweiler's Used Books, on Second Avenue. According to Mrs. Dockweiler, it had been her husband's custom, summer and winter, to walk through Central Park each night from their shop to their apartment on West Eighty-third Street.

Mrs. Dockweiler had told the *Times* reporter that often she'd warned her husband that Central Park was dangerous, particularly after nightfall. "But he always told me that lots of shopkeepers and businessmen get their exercise that way, walking home through the park, and there was no danger as long as you stayed on the lighted paths. Maybe he got confused by the snowfall. Or maybe it was his being so sick. The doctors had given him only a few more months to live."

Oblivious of two giggling girls who, a few feet away, had opened another volume, Karen read on.

So far, she read, police had been unable to locate anyone who recalled hearing shots or any sound of struggle that night, even though they'd questioned their own personnel on park duty at the time, and Parks Department employees, and a group of eastside dog owners who'd often been observed in the early evenings at a spot about two hundred yards east of where the body had been found.

Lifting her gaze, Karen stared unseeingly at the opposite wall. She could imagine how each of them had looked as he or she told the agreed-upon lies to the police. May Cosgrove, gentle-faced and gentle-voiced, and no doubt offering the detective a cup of tea. The Kinsings, presenting such a picture of upper-middle-class respectability in their penthouse apartment that the detective must have questioned them briefly and politely indeed. Consuelo, fixing her interrogator with a cold brown stare as she denied seeing anything, hearing anything. Henry Maize, no doubt looking frightened— Karen had often seen what appeared to be some chronic anxiety in his eyes—but so obviously a quiet, lonely man living the dullest of lives, that the detective must have felt inclined to make the questioning as easy for him as possible.

In the case of Paul Winship, with his pseudo-hipness, his malice that he seemed unable to hide for more than a few minutes, the questioning may have been a little rougher. Still, apparently he'd been able to convince the police that for him, too, the gathering on the hill the night of January tenth had been uneventful.

That left David. Handsome, charming, almost-famous David, whom it would be hard to suspect of suppressing evidence in the death of an obscure old man, let alone perpetrating that death.

Lowering her eyes to the page, Karen read the final sentence, "The slain man left no other immediate survivors."

For several minutes she searched through subsequent issues of the paper. No mention of Herman Dockweiler. Evidently any information that might have led to the man's slayer had remained hidden from official eyes, like the vanished gun, like the snow-buried footprints around the body.

"But you have that information," an inner voice said, "don't you?" Closing the volume, she hurried out to the sidewalk.

Already the gray daylight was fading. Neon signs were on now, smears of red and green and blue light through the steadily falling snow. A half block from the *Times* building, she turned into a small restaurant, intending to order just coffee. But when she saw a sign behind the counter, "No order less than fifty cents," she remembered that she hadn't had lunch, and ordered a cheese sandwich.

The sandwich looked fresh enough. It was her own inner conflict that made the food seem dry and tasteless. Illogically, perhaps, she'd hoped to find something in the paper that would end her conflict, something that would force her to go to the police immediately or, conversely, justify her in doing what she really wanted to do—turn her back on it, forget it, let David's fate rest in any other hands but hers.

The newspaper account, though, hadn't helped at all. True, it had given her one extra bit of information, the name of the Dockweiler shop on Second Avenue. Had Mrs. Dockweiler kept the store open? Perhaps. Few widows of secondhand booksellers could afford to live in idleness.

Abandoning her half-eaten sandwich, she walked back to a phone booth and looked through a dog-eared copy of the classified directory. The Dockweiler shop, she found, was at an address on Second Avenue very close to Consuelo Bryant's photographic studio. Well, that couldn't he helped, and anyway, Consuelo probably wouldn't see her.

Going back to the counter, she left fifteen cents beside her plate. She paid her bill at the cashier's desk. Outside the café snow still fell fast and thick, perhaps even more thickly than that night in Central Park nearly a month ago, into the neon-lighted canyon of Forty-fourth Street.

19

David Bryant stood motionless at the window of his lamp-lit living room. Snow falling through the early dusk outside sharpened his reflection in the windowpane. He could see the stubble on his chin and a split in the shoulder seam of the old navy blue dressing gown he wore.

Upon returning to his apartment the night before, he'd followed May Cosgrove's advice to Karen, and flushed the little candies away, two and three at a time. Then he'd taken the empty box and its wrappings out into the hall and dropped them down the incinerator chute.

As he turned back to his apartment, he tried to hold onto a momentary sense of relief, But it was no use. True, he'd disposed of one clear and present danger, the poison May Cosgrove had injected into those candies. But there could be no such easy disposal of the knowledge she'd injected into Karen's mind.

He'd sat up until past four in the morning, drinking Scotch and water. The alcohol, he'd hoped, would relax him to the point where he could make some infallible plan for escaping the doom he felt closing in on him. Instead, the drinks had only reinforced his paralyzing mood of despair and useless regret.

Since one-thirty that afternoon, when he'd awakened with a bad hangover, he'd telephoned Karen's apartment repeatedly, without receiving an answer. Where was she? Had she taken that candy to the police? If so, he hoped the Crime Lab had analyzed it promptly and given her their negative report. He also hoped that the police hadn't been too inquisitive about her reason for wanting it analyzed. He doubted that they had been. New York was a city where detectives sometimes worked thirty hours at a stretch trying to cope not only with burgeoning crime, but with assorted nuts who thought their neighbors were assaulting them with gamma rays, or piping carbon monoxide into their bedrooms, or stealthily opening their refrigerators to add arsenic to leftover tapioca pudding. No, the police wouldn't let her and her marzipan take up any more time than necessary.

Unless, of course, she'd told them that she suspected her former almost-fiancé of trying to poison her. But she wouldn't do that, not unless she was prepared to tell them why she suspected him. And if she'd done that, if she'd repeated to them the story told to her by May Cosgrove, he'd already have heard the sounds he'd been dreading all afternoon—the buzzer from downstairs, and a voice on the intercom saying, "Mr. Bryant? Mr. David Bryant? This is the police."

No, she must still be hesitating, still trying to resolve her own conflict. If only he could get to her before she decided the wrong way. If he could do that, then he'd have a chance of keeping her silent, either by pleading with her, or . . . Nausea tightening his stomach, he blotted out a vision of Karen's crumpled body.

You heard of cold-blooded murderers, planning their crimes as unemotionally as a chicken farmer might plan how best to destroy a marauding fox. Undoubtedly some people did kill like that. But David had a feeling that many murders, even premeditated ones, were carried out by men like himself. Men who killed with revulsion, and out of fear. As he had killed Herman Dockweiler, and as he had tried to kill Karen.

Had he been planning his act, even as they went down the subway steps? He didn't know. Probably he had been, at least on a subconscious level. But all he could be sure of was that, when he saw her leaning out over the platform's edge, thoughts had flashed through his mind: "She's become suspicious, and therefore dangerous. But if she dies right now . . ."

And yet he hadn't really wanted to see Karen, lovely Karen, mangled by that steel monster. When he caught sight of the two strangers hurrying down the platform, and knew he'd have to reach down and pull her to safety, a sense of reprieve had mingled with his terror.

Weeks ago, he should have done something about Karen. Perhaps he should have written her a letter so brutal that, if she'd returned to New York at all, it would have been with no thought of seeing him. Or perhaps he should have followed her down to Raleigh and asked her to marry him. Instead, fearful of making a mistake, he'd done nothing, which had turned out to be the worst mistake of all.

No, that wasn't true. The worst mistake, the one that had brought him to this moment when he stood staring at his ghostly, unshaven reflection in the windowpane, had been the fundamental one. And he'd made that one spring day nearly two years before.

It had been a beautiful afternoon, with a tender blue sky arching overhead, and trees on the cross streets unfurling pale green leaves, and the fragrance of hyacinths wafting from corner flower stands. But his mood hadn't matched the day. As he walked toward his sister's Second Avenue studio, with Britt padding beside him, he had a gloomy awareness that he was about to muff the biggest opportunity that had come his way so far. The producers of *The Blue Planet,* a children's TV special scheduled for presentation in late summer, had asked him to submit suitable theme music. He'd been delighted, because he'd heard via the grapevine that

The Blue Planet was shaping up as a smash, the kind that boosts the reputation of everyone involved in its making.

They'd given him until the first of May. After that, they'd turn to another composer. It was now April twenty-fourth. Deep in one of those creative slumps that sometimes afflicted him he'd been unable to come up with anything that wasn't either too banal for a prestige show or too difficult for a young audience.

He spent an irritating forty minutes with Consuelo, who'd insisted upon his posing for some new publicity photos that afternoon, even though he'd told her the night before that he was in no mood for a sitting. When he emerged from her studio, he stood there on the sidewalk for a moment, knowing he should try to work, but unwilling to return to his apartment and that wastebasket beside the piano, half-filled with crumpled pages, each bearing a few bars of music.

His gaze found a shop window sign almost directly across the street. "The Melbourne Shop. Used Books." Smaller letters beneath said, "Herman Dockweiler, Prop." With Britt beside him, he made an illegal crossing in the middle of the block. The nice thing about secondhand bookstores was that the proprietors never asked what you were looking for. In fact, most of them seemed to ignore you, unless and until you brought some purchase to them. And David was in no mood for conversation.

The proprietor of this particular shop, though, a thin, elderly man seated behind a paper-strewn desk at the far end of the narrow room, proved to be unusually chatty. He said, peering at David over the tops of his granny glasses, "That's a fine-looking animal you've got there. But how can a dog that size get enough exercise in the city?"

"She gets enough," David said shortly. Then, because he'd found it good policy to be pleasant whenever possible, he added, "She gets a run in Central Park every night, and sometimes in the afternoon, too."

The old man nodded. "Great place, Central Park. I walk

home through it to the westside every night. My wife—she goes home first, most nights, to start dinner—my wife doesn't like me to, what with all the muggers and such these days. But I've been walking through that park, night and morning, for thirty years, and I'm damned if I'll stop now."

"I can see how you'd feel that way," David said, and turned his attention to a long table laden with tightly packed rows of books, their spines turned upward. He began to move along the table, picking up a book now and then and leafing through a few pages before he replaced it. Once, hearing a door open, he glanced up and saw a plump, white-haired woman with thick-lensed glasses come into the shop from some back room, a feather duster in her hand.

He was more than halfway through the rows of books before he noticed the cardboard box sitting there at the table's end. It was just an ordinary packing box which once, according to the lettering on its side, had held canned milk. Moving to it, he found that now it was filled halfway to the top with sheet music of the sort that, when the century was young, had rested on piano music racks all over the world.

Temporarily diverted from his worry, he began to remove the folded sheets one by one from the box, laying them atop the rows of books. "Shine On, Harvest Moon," with buxom Nora Bayes on the cover. "Buy Me a Bow-wow," with a photograph of sloe-eyed Anna Held. "After the Ball Is Over," with its mustached composer on the cover. Perhaps two dozen of these reminders that, back in the days when there were no magic boxes to bring a disk jockey's voice or a comedian's face into the living room, families gathered around pianos to create their own home entertainment.

At the bottom of the box lay a flat book with its title, *Piano Exercises,* printed in tarnished gilt on its green cover. Piano exercises didn't interest him. He was about to turn back to the pile of sheet music when he saw, protruding from between the bottom edges of the stiff green covers, part of a page of music, hand-written in faded brown ink. Curious now, he took *Piano Exercises* from the box and opened it.

Across the top of the sheet of music, neatly printed in that same brown ink, was the title, "Lost in Love's Dream." Beneath that the composer had printed his name, Charles Brownlow, and the place and date of composition, Melbourne, Australia, 1901. The composer, or at least someone, had written a lyric for the music.

Ignoring the words, David concentrated on the notes. Before he read more than a few bars, he felt his heart begin to pound. Here it was, the perfect music for *The Blue Planet*, the sort of music he'd been trying to wring from his own brain. It was exactly right. Melodic, but not banal. Simple, but not simple-minded, not with those unexpected but exactly right minors. He reread it, mentally orchestrating it now, hearing in his mind's ear the first crystal notes of a piano stating the theme, and then the woodwinds coming in, and the brasses. And right here, a sitar, perhaps? Yes, a sitar.

This music had never been published. If it had been, David would have been familiar with it. The date of its composition was probably the reason for its failure to find a publisher. This Charles Brownlow, whoever he was, had been ahead of his time. Around the turn of the century, no one was offering songs like this one to the public. Orchestral music, yes. Debussy, for instance. But not popular songs. And Charles Brownlow had meant his composition to be a popular song. The lyric testified to that, the almost incredibly trite lyric: "My sweetheart and I, 'neath an azure blue sky, walk by a stream, lost in love's dream." Brownlow's talent had been strictly musical. Otherwise he'd never have written those words or allowed anyone else to attach them to his lovely music.

His music. Unpublished music written by a man on the other side of the world nearly three-quarters of a century ago, a man surely dead by now. Music that David Bryant should have written, music he almost felt he *had* written.

Feeling someone's gaze upon him, he looked up. The old man was regarding him. The woman, dusting a heavy book she'd taken down from a shelf, was also looking at him through her thick-lensed glasses. Until he felt that leap of guilt, David hadn't actually known what he was going to do. But now he knew.

Casually, he lowered his gaze to the single sheet of music spread out on one page of the exercise book. Could they, at that distance, tell that he'd been studying a sheet of paper slightly longer than the pages of the book itself? Probably not. With seeming indifference, he closed the book and placed it back in the box. Then he turned to the pile of sheet music, laying a few pieces aside, but restoring most of them to the box. "Lost in Love's Dream" soon lay hidden, not just by the covers of the exercise book, but by about two dozen songs of pre-World War One vintage. It also lay in David's memory, every note of it. Picking up the three pieces of sheet music he'd laid aside, he walked back to the desk.

"You see, Irma," the proprietor said, "I told you people buy things like old sheet music these days. Camp, they call it. Isn't that right, young fellow?"

David smiled. "That's right."

"My wife insisted on bringing tons of stuff like that from Australia with us. That old sheet music has been down in the storeroom ever since we opened this shop, thirty years ago. I told her a month ago I was going to bring it upstairs, because there was a market for it."

"Some market," his wife said. "This is the first you've sold of it." She softened the words by smiling, first at her husband, and then at David. David returned her smile.

"That's better than not selling any at all," her husband retorted.

Outwardly relaxed, but inwardly wild with impatience,

David watched the man lay the sheet music on a rectangle of green paper, slowly roll it into a cylinder, and tie it with white string.

"How much do I owe you?"

"Oh, let's say sixty cents, plus tax."

David's long stride had carried him four blocks through the late afternoon light before it occurred to him that perhaps he should have contrived, somehow, to bring Charles Brownlow's composition with him. He should have devised some means of distracting their attention long enough to slip it into his pocket. Or perhaps he should have bought the whole box of junk, and then told them that he'd carry it away just as it was, since he had his car parked around the corner.

Halting, he looked at his watch. Too late to go back now. In all probability, the shop would be closed. Well, tomorrow would do. Neither the proprietor nor his wife would be likely to look through the box, since they knew, or at least thought they knew, all that it contained. And if that old sheet music had been there a month without attracting customers, it was most unlikely that anyone would even browse through it tomorrow, let alone open the exercise book. And what if someone did? How many customers would be able even to read that music, let alone recognize its quality? To ninety-nine out of a hundred people, Charles Brownlow's composition would be an old piece of paper, covered with unreadable musical notes and with someone's lame attempt at lyric writing.

With an orchestra playing inside his head, he hurried on through the sunset light to his apartment.

He didn't return to the shop the next day, or the next, or the next. So obsessed by his music—it seemed to him completely his now—that he scarcely stopped to eat, he completed the entire orchestration of *The Blue Planet Theme*. Late on the third afternoon, he took it down to the TV producer's duplex apartment on West Twelfth Street and played it on the piano. When he emerged into the tree-lined street, with the producer's praises echoing in his mind, he had an intoxicated sense that if the whole world wasn't his right now, it soon would be.

The next morning he returned to the Melbourne Shop, only to find the door padlocked and a sign pasted to its upper pane of opaque glass: "Closed because of illness."

As David turned away, an old man wielding a broom outside the cubbyhole tobacco shop next door said, "Mr. Dockweiler's in the hospital."

"The man who runs the bookstore?"

"That's right. Doctors operated this morning." His broom sent cigarette stubs and a candy wrapper flying into the gutter. "He kept getting these stomach pains, see. Everybody kept telling him to go to the doctor. His wife told him, *I* told him. Finally one day last week he did go. When the doctor saw the X-rays, he hustled him right into the hospital."

David said mechanically, "I hope he gets well," and walked on. It was all right, he told himself. As long as the shop remained closed, it was all right.

Every few days during May, June, and July, he checked the Melbourne Shop. The place remained padlocked. Then, one morning in August, he found the door standing wide open. One swift glance as he passed showed him that Herman Dockweiler, thinner than ever, sat bent over his desk. It also showed him that the cardboard box no longer stood on the book-laden table.

As he strode toward the corner, he debated turning back. He could ask if there was any of that old sheet music left. . . . No, he decided. Leafing casually through that box, if it had still been there, wouldn't have aroused the old man's interest. But asking to have it brought up from the basement, or wherever it had been placed, might provoke a hovering attention that would prevent him from slipping "Lost in Love's Dream" into his pocket. He'd have to leave it there. And later the proprietor, his curiosity aroused, might go carefully through the box, find the hand-written music, and begin to wonder. . . .

And anyway, the box and its contents were probably no longer in the Dockweilers' possession. Probably, feeling that the sheet music had aroused too little interest to warrant giving it shoproom, they'd put the box out for the trash collectors. Yes, that was it, that must be it. Perhaps even before Mr. Dockweiler's operation, that sheet of paper with musical notes written in faded brown ink had been carried on a scow into the Atlantic, and dumped fathoms deep.

For a fleeting moment, he realized that he'd been rationalizing. The truth was that he feared entering that shop, and returning in time to that spring afternoon. During the past weeks, he'd been able to feel, at least most of the time, that the music was his own. He didn't want to relive those moments when, with admiration and burning envy, he'd been completely aware that the composition in his hands was another man's.

Then he thrust the realization from him. It was just, he told himself, that it was better to leave well enough alone.

Because by that time things were going very well indeed. In late July, *The Blue Planet* had been presented. The reviews, all enthusiastic, had singled David out for special praise. A record company was bringing out a David Bryant album which would offer not only *The Blue Planet Theme*, but other compositions which, with a new self-confidence born of success, he'd written since last May. And there were the TV awards coming up. . . .

To no one's surprise, including his, he won the award for best musical theme.

For more than a year after that, life seemed like a doting maiden aunt, determined to do its best by David Bryant. His album enjoyed a steady though modest sale. He wrote musical themes for three more TV shows. None of them attracted as much attention as *The Blue Planet Theme*, but the reviews were favorable, and the fees nice indeed. He appeared several times on TV talk shows. And, one September night, a girl had joined the little group of dog owners on the hill, a girl with long-lashed, hazel eyes, and a North Carolina accent, and a dog named Bozo.

On the afternoon of the previous January tenth, he was feeling especially content. Karen would be back from Raleigh soon. The night before, *The Blue Planet* had been presented for the second time. And beyond his window the winter's first heavy snow—almost as heavy as that falling beyond his unshaven reflection now—had descended through the waning afternoon light. The storm seemed to increase his sense of warm well-being and his pleasure in the Vivaldi recording he'd placed on the hi-fi.

The phone rang. Feeling annoyed, he shut off the music and lifted the handset. "Hello."

A vaguely familiar voice said, "Mr. Bryant? Mr. David Bryant?"

"Speaking."

"This is Herman Dockweiler, Mr. Bryant. I run the Melbourne Bookshop."

The lampglow in the room had seemed to alter, taking on the cold shine of the light that illuminates a bad dream.

"You're a thief, Mr. Bryant. You stole the music for that TV show I saw last night."

David heard his own voice, sounding unnaturally calm. "I don't know what you're talking about."

"Oh, yes, you do. My wife's uncle wrote that music years before I even met her. He used to play it for me when I was courting Irma, and I never forgot it."

David stood mute. After a moment Herman Dockweiler went on, "When I opened the shop today, I went down to the basement and looked in that box of old sheet music. Nobody but you had ever shown much interest in it, so I lugged the box back down there—oh, summer before last, right after I got out of the hospital. I found Charlie Brownlow's song in that old exercise book, the one you looked at so long the day you were in here."

David managed to move his lips. "Where is it now?"

"That song? In a safe place, Mr. Bryant. A safe place."

"Why—why did you wait so long? *The Blue Planet* was first shown over a year ago—"

"So I see by the papers. But I didn't see the show then because I was in the hospital. My wife didn't see it either. For one thing, she doesn't watch TV much. For another, our set had broken down, and we were pretty hard up right then, and—well, that's neither here nor there. The point is, I didn't see the show until last night."

"Did your wife see it?"

"No. I told you. She doesn't watch TV much. Too hard on the eyes, she says. Anyway, she'd gone to an Altar Society meeting."

"But you've told her—?"

"No. My wife's a high-strung woman, and she was fond of her Uncle Charlie. I don't want her to know anything about it until it's all settled."

Settled. David said, his voice hardening, "How much?"

"Just money won't settle it, Mr. Bryant. Oh, not that my wife isn't going to need money after—"

He broke off, and then went on, "But what I really want is justice. My wife's uncle was a nice man, and he never got anywhere. He tried and tried, but he never sold a note of his music. It doesn't seem fair that someone else—"

"Just what do you want?"

"Well, we can work out the money part of it. I guess some of it belongs to you. As I understand it, there's a lot of work to fixing up music for various instruments, and so on. But the main credit doesn't belong to you, Mr. Bryant. It belongs to Charles Brownlow, even though he's been dead for forty years now. I want him to have it, that's all."

All. All he wanted was for David to ruin himself utterly, to brand himself as a thief before the whole world. All his music would become suspect then. There'd be no more TV assignments, no more talk shows, no more awards.

"Mr. Bryant, are you still there?"

It was an effort to speak. "Yes."

"I want to see you about this, right today."

Stall. Fight for time—time to think. "I can't, Mr. Dockweiler. I'm expecting a—a music publisher at any moment. And this evening—"

"Mr. Bryant, you've got no choice. I don't want to be any harder on you than I have to. But if we can't settle this right away, I'm going to court. I've got proof, absolute proof, that the music you claim is yours was written years and years before you were born. If I'm crowding you, Mr. Bryant, it's because I haven't much time. I mean, there's been a recurrence, and this time an operation won't—"

He stopped for a moment and then went on, "I'm not asking for a financial settlement right today. But I do want a written statement from you, admitting that Charles Brownlow wrote that music, and just when and how you stole it."

David stared blindly at a picture on the wall, a framed Toulouse-Lautrec poster which some girl had given him several years before. Quite another picture was taking shape in his thoughts.

"All right, Mr. Dockweiler, I'll give you that statement, but not here. I'll meet you somewhere," He paused. "I don't suppose you'll be walking home through the park this evening, not with all this snow."

"You suppose wrong. I like snow, and I like the park, and I'm going to enjoy both every minute I can."

"Do you know the playing field about two hundred yards west of the museum?"

"I do."

"I'll meet you there, at a quarter of seven."

"Where in the playing field? It's a pretty big area, Mr. Bryant."

"Well, you know that backstop at the western end of it?

147

It's about sixty or seventy feet off the path. How about there?"

"All right, quarter of seven. Don't forget the statement, Mr. Bryant."

Herman Dockweiler hung up. David stood there a moment, the phone still in his hand. Then he replaced the phone, went into the bedroom, and opened his top bureau drawer. There it was, the little twenty-two pistol which wasn't registered anyplace, because his father had bought it many years ago, before there were gun registration laws. If he avoided fingerprints, there'd be no reason why he couldn't just leave it there, in the park.

Almost three hours later, waiting near the backstop in the dark playing field with Britt sitting quietly beside him, he'd seen a dim figure approaching through the snow curtain. Hearing the pound of his own heart, like the beat of storm-driven surf, he asked, "Mr. Dockweiler?"

"That's right, Mr. Bryant." The figure drew close. "Have you brought that statement?"

David shot him three times, through the heart.

Then, just as he'd been about to drop the gun and turn away, he'd heard Henry Maize call out. There he was, he and that cocker spaniel of his, looming through the snowflakes.

During the next few moments, while Henry Maize knelt beside the body, David hadn't had to fake hysteria. He'd sobbed in genuine despair. But as the older man led him, still sobbing, toward that group on the hill, his mind began to function again.

Henry—old hit-and-run Henry—would keep quiet about this if David told him to. Could he persuade the others? Perhaps. With the exception of George Kinsing and May Cosgrove, each of them had at least some reason to help him. And maybe even those two . . .

Tell them it had all been an accident. He hadn't even known the man he shot. He'd arranged to meet someone he

148

was afraid of. Someone who was trying to get money from him, that was it. Someone like that broken-down trombonist who, when David had run into him on Madison Avenue, had returned ten dollars to him.

Perhaps he'd have given them another name than Slide Thompson's, some fictitious name, if he'd had more time to think. But by then he stood in their midst, dimly aware of shocked faces, of May Cosgrove's twittering cries, of Consuelo's voice, harsh and bullying, as it always was when she became frightened.

They'd believed the story. Perhaps his low, ragged sobs, which he couldn't seem to stop, helped convince them. And when Consuelo demanded fiercely that they all "keep quiet about this for twenty-four hours," they'd all agreed, Doris Kinsing and May Cosgrove without hesitation, the others less promptly. As he'd expected, Henry Maize had finally said in a dull voice, "All right." Paul Winship, with some sly remark about being fellow composers, had also assented. George Kinsing had held out for a while, saying that since it had been, in a sense, an accident, the law wouldn't punish David too severely. And when the police questioned them, as they almost surely would, they mustn't, they just mustn't, withhold evidence.

Then Doris had shaken his arm hard. "George," she said, her voice heavy with some obscure threat, "You'd *better.*"

George had looked down into his wife's face for a long moment, and then said, in a quiet voice, "All right."

And May Cosgrove, who for some reason known only to her batty self seemed not only willing but eager to protect him, had held out her hand and offered to dispose of the gun.

Early the next afternoon, a bright, sunny one, two detectives had visited David. Nerves soothed with sedatives, he'd been ready for them.

No, he said, he'd heard no shots in the park the night before.

Had he taken his dog to that playing field west of the museum last night? They were asking, one of them explained, because the movie scooter policeman who'd recognized him from his TV appearances had also reported that Mr. Bryant sometimes took his dog over to that field.

"Not last night," David said. "It was snowing too damned hard. Why do you ask?"

They explained then that Herman Dockweiler's body had been found in that field. "We thought if you'd gone to the field, you might have seen or heard something."

"Oh, I understand. Sorry I can't help."

At their request, he'd given them the names of the others in the little group of dog owners. They'd thanked him, and left.

He and Consuelo had been the first ones on the hill that night. Then the Kinsings had arrived, and right behind them Paul Winship. A few minutes later May Cosgrove, with Henry Maize holding her arm, had toiled up the slope through the previous night's snowfall. Scanning each face in turn, David knew even before they spoke that they'd kept silent. He also felt reasonably sure that they'd agree to remain silent. The stories in the afternoon paper, saying that the old man would have been dead within a few months anyway, must have eased their consciences somewhat. But the chief reason he could hope to keep them silent was that they realized they were in this with him now, not as deep as he was, but deep enough. He could read that realization in Paul Winship's uneasy smile, and the accentuated slump of Henry Maize's shoulders, and the grim resignation on George Kinsing's face. Even his sister's manner seemed subdued. Only May Cosgrove, whose brains were addled, and Doris Kinsing, who'd never had any brains to speak of, seemed unaware of the seriousness of their situation.

He told them the plan he'd worked out. In a few weeks, just as soon as he felt he could do so without attracting official attention, he'd go to Europe, perhaps permanently.

"But in the meantime," Consuelo said, "We'll continue to meet up here. If we don't, it would look—funny."

George Kinsing said, in a flat, hopeless voice, "Yes, that's what we'd better do."

For David the weeks since then had held constant strain. Strain of trying to work. Strain of turning on the charm whenever he appeared on a TV show. And the strain of dealing with those who held not only his career but his freedom in their hands. Paul Winship and his crummy songs. May Cosgrove and her invitations to have "little chats." Doris Kinsing and her quite different invitations, which would be dangerous to accept and even more dangerous to ignore, and so had to be met with smiles blending amorousness and wry regret, smiles that said, "If only you weren't another man's wife . . ."

Still, he'd managed to hold up pretty well until last Monday night, when he'd seen Bozo scrambling up the hill, and had known Karen was back in town. At sight of that dog, he'd felt a silent screaming within him.

Karen. Where was she?

Turning from his unshaven reflection in the windowpane, he walked to the phone, dialed. Still no answer.

He started back to the window, and then halted. It was crazy to stand there staring at himself in the pane. He'd better shower, shave, dress, and drown the remnants of his hangover in hot coffee. Then, when Karen finally answered her phone, he'd be ready to hurry over to her place.

Turning, he walked toward the bathroom.

20

When Karen entered the bookshop, the white-haired woman seated behind a desk at the far end looked up. With the overhead lights glinting on her thick-lensed glasses, she smiled at Karen and then lowered her gaze to the ledger spread out before her.

For a moment Karen just stood there, looking around her at the book-lined walls, the long table bearing more books. She had no clear idea of what she sought. She'd only felt that there might be something here—something that would indicate whether or not David had ever known Herman Dockweiler.

Well, the first thing to do was to try to find out if David had ever been in this shop. As Karen moved forward, the woman looked up with a faintly surprised expression. "Something I can help you with, dear?"

"I was wondering if you could tell me whether or not a friend of mine has been in here recently. He's about thirty, and six-feet-two inches tall, and has very pale blond hair."

The woman smiled. "Sounds like a movie star."

Karen returned the smile. "Oh, he's not an actor, but he has been a guest on TV shows."

"Well, I don't watch TV. I have to save my eyesight for the shop. But I'm sure the young man you mean was in here once—oh, sometime the spring before last. I remember it wasn't many days before my husband went to the hospital—"

She broke off, and then added, in an altered tone, "My husband was killed about a month ago. Someone shot him in Central Park. Maybe you read about it. His name was Herman Dockweiler."

After a moment Karen was able to say, "I'm very sorry to hear that, Mrs. Dockweiler."

"It seemed so senseless." For a moment the eyes behind the thick lenses held an expression of puzzled pain. Then she straightened her shoulders slightly and said, "But about your friend. As far as I know, he was in here only once."

Karen tried to make her voice casual. "Did he buy many books?"

"He didn't buy any. He just bought three pieces of sheet music from that box over there. That's the reason I remember your friend—that and his good looks, of course."

Turning, Karen followed the direction of the woman's gaze. A cardboard box, she saw now, sat at one end of the book-laden table.

"What I mean is," Mrs. Dockweiler said, "my husband was so sure that old music would sell. But your friend was the only one who ever showed any interest in it, so after my husband reopened the shop—it was closed while he was in the hospital and for a while afterwards—he lugged the box down to the cellar."

"But now you've brought it up again."

"Yes, just the other day. I unlocked the storage closet in the basement and found it. Why my husband put it under lock and key, I don't know. But anyway, I decided to offer it for sale again. I mean, with business so slow, even an extra dollar here and there—"

Her voice trailed off. Karen said, "I'd like to look at it."

"Go right ahead, dear." Mrs. Dockweiler returned her attention to the ledger.

Moving to the box, Karen began lifting out gaudily covered sheet music. "I'm a Yankee Doodle Dandy," "Juanita," "Tell Me, Pretty Maiden." Would David have called this low camp or high camp? Either way, he'd have been amused by it. No doubt that was the only reason the contents of this box had caught his attention. Nevertheless, still on that vague search, she opened each piece of sheet music before she laid it aside.

Nothing in the box now except a flat book bound in green cloth and entitled *Piano Exercises*. She lifted it out, opened it. A song, or at least what someone apparently had hoped was a song, written in faded brown ink.

She began to read the notes.

After a while she closed her eyes for an appalled second, opened them, and read the composition through again. There could be no doubt. It was *The Blue Planet Theme*, bar for bar, note for note.

Here it was in her hand, proof of a theft which had brought David many thousands of dollars and—far more important to his career in the long run—wide critical acclaim. A proof which Herman Dockweiler had discovered and locked away in a basement closet.

David hadn't thought he was confronting some drug-addicted extortionist in the park that night. He'd known he was facing an old man, feeble, and yet with the power to destroy his career.

Not accidental homicide, she thought numbly. Murder— deliberate murder.

She placed the sheet music back in the box. Then, carrying the exercise book in one hand and Charles Brownlow's composition in the other, she walked over to the desk.

"Mrs. Dockweiler." The woman looked up. Karen laid the book and the page of music on the desk. "I found this song in that old exercise book."

"Why, for heaven's sake!" Mrs. Dockweiler said. "My Uncle Charlie wrote that song. I remember the title and the words. It must have been lying in that book for maybe forty years. Probably my mother put it in there after Uncle Charlie died."

154

"Mrs. Dockweiler, put that music away. Lock it up. It's made lots of money, and probably will make more. Unless your uncle had other heirs, that money belongs to you."

Mrs. Dockweiler started at her blankly. "Dear, you're mistaken. That song never made a cent. None of Uncle Charlie's songs were ever published. He couldn't seem to understand why, but the rest of us could, even though we weren't what you could call a musical family. A love song has to have a pretty tune, and his never did."

"Just the same, this one song of your uncle's made a lot of money."

And cost your husband the last months of his life. But of course she wouldn't say that. Mrs. Dockweiler would find that out soon enough. "Please lock it up, Mrs. Dockweiler."

She turned. Aware that the woman must be looking after her in blank astonishment, she hurried toward the sidewalk.

For a few seconds after the door closed behind the girl, Mrs. Dockweiler went on staring at it. What a pity. There must be something definitely wrong with the girl. And she'd seemed such a nice little thing.

She looked down at the sheet of music written in faded ink. How could "Lost in Love's Dream" have made a lot of money, when it had never been published, when it had lain tucked away in an old book for the Lord only knew how long?

Nevertheless, it wouldn't hurt to . . .

Opening the top drawer of the desk, she took out keys, unlocked a lower drawer, and put the sheet of paper in it. When she'd relocked the drawer, she carried the exercise book back to the cardboard box. Lifting out the sheet music —better to keep the more eye-catching items on top—she laid the exercise book in the bottom of the box.

You never could tell. Somebody interested enough in piano music to look through those old songs might like to buy a book of piano exercises.

21

David was brushing his hair at the bathroom mirror when the phone rang. Laying the brush down, he moved swiftly into the living room and picked up the handset.

"David, Karen Wentworth's been in that bookshop!" Consuelo's voice was harsh with anxiety. "I was standing at the front door a minute ago, and I saw her come out of the shop and turn up the street—"

"So what?" Despite the panicky leap of his heart, he tried to make his voice soothingly calm, lest his sister's alarm heighten his own. "Why shouldn't she go into a bookshop? The girl's literate."

"David! Don't you understand? She was in Herman Dock-weiler's shop."

Like the others, Consuelo had seemed to accept his statement that the man he'd shot had been a complete stranger to him. But now, and not for the first time, he wondered if she'd really believed him.

"All right. I'll check to see what she was up to." Before Consuelo could answer, he replaced the phone in its cradle.

He glanced at his watch. Not quite five. He'd have time to walk over to the bookshop. Still fighting for calm, he went back to the bathroom and picked up the brush.

Coincidence? Perhaps. Karen liked secondhand bookshops, just as he did. They'd spent one whole Saturday afternoon last fall browsing through the bookstores along Astor Place.

And even if it wasn't coincidence, what could she learn? Nothing from Dockweiler's widow, certainly. If she'd had any idea of why her husband was killed, she'd have told the police long ago.

Then why was his hand trembling?

Looking up from her ledger, Mrs. Dockweiler stared at the man who'd just come in. Why, it was that handsome young man, the one the girl had been asking about not half an hour ago. He moved toward her, smiling. And then, to Mrs. Dockweiler's bewilderment, he stopped short, staring at that old cardboard box, staring at it as if it were—well, a ghost or something.

He was moving toward her again, smiling so pleasantly that she almost felt she'd imagined that look on his face. "Hello," he said. "I wonder if you can tell me whether or not a friend of mine has been in here today. She's brown-haired, pretty—"

Mrs. Dockweiler laughed. "What are you two up to? Is it some kind of game?" She tilted her head roguishly. "Or maybe a lovers' quarrel?"

David managed an embarrassed smile. "Something like that. So she was in here." His voice took on a hopeful note. "Did she buy any books? I mean, before we had our row yesterday, she asked what I wanted for my birthday, and I mentioned this book that's out of print."

"I'm sorry. She didn't buy anything."

"Or even look at anything?"

"Well, she did seem sort of interested in the old sheet music in that box, but maybe that was only because I told her you'd bought some of it the other time you were in here."

Under his overcoat and suit jacket and shirt, he felt cold sweat roll down his sides. So it was the same box. After that first bad moment, he'd told himself that it couldn't be, that the world was full of old cardboard boxes that had once held canned milk. But there it was, the same box, like some god-damned albatross.

He had an almost overwhelming need to rush to the box, paw through it. But he mustn't. He must be casual about it. Plainly the woman was already puzzled, perhaps even a little suspicious. He said in that same hopeful tone, "Did she buy any of the sheet music?"

"No. But she did find something else in the box. It was the most amazing thing. She walked over and handed me this song that an uncle of mine wrote before I was born! It wasn't sheet music. Poor Uncle Charlie never had anything pub—"

She broke off, frightened. There was something in his face . . .

He smiled and said, "Could I see it? Maybe it sounds funny, but I'm hipped on pre-World War One stuff, ragtime pianos, and old postcards, and old sheet music."

It was silly to have felt frightened. He was such a nice, handsome young man, and plainly very upset about his fight with his girl. Surely that was why his manner seemed odd. Just the same, better not show him Uncle Charlie's song. There was just a chance that the girl might have been right about its being valuable And she was alone in the shop.

"I can't show it to you. Your friend bought it."

"Bought it?"

He was looking strange again, his face green-white. She said, suddenly wanting very much to get rid of him, "She offered me fifty cents for it, so I let her have it." Pointedly, she looked down at the ledger. When she again looked up, he was striding toward the door.

Out on the sidewalk, he turned north. The snow, which had slackened somewhat while he was on his way from his apartment to the bookstore, was now coming down more thickly than ever. He knew that Consuelo must be standing behind the glass-paned door of her studio, trying to catch a glimpse of him through the thick white smother. But he had no time to talk to Consuelo. The faint crunch of his striding footsteps seemed to echo that. No time, no time, no time.

And only one hope. No chance now that he could persuade Karen to keep quiet. All he could do now, he thought, still wearing that face which had frightened Mrs. Dockweiler, was to try to get to Karen before she got to the police.

But first he had to get hold of a gun. Better, far better, if he'd risked keeping that unregistered twenty-two of his father's. It was only because he'd feared alienating her that he'd let May Cosgrove take it that night. No telling what she'd done with it, and no time to coax the batty old girl into telling him. ("No time," his footsteps agreed, crunching over rock salt strewn for a few yards over a freshly shoveled sidewalk.) He'd have to try to buy a gun in that First Avenue pawnshop and then get rid of it. Afterwards.

At the corner, he turned right toward First Avenue.

22

Just do it, Karen told herself, hurrying the last few yards toward the steps of her apartment house. Just get out of these wet clothes, and then call the police. And stop thinking about the past. Above all, don't think about last New Year's Eve, and the beech tree against the North Carolina sky, and those visions of David and herself and two children with lemon-yellow hair in a house on a green Connecticut hill.

The David she'd loved had never existed. Always the real David must have been, potentially, the one who'd coldly fired three bullets into an old man's heart.

She was moving along the lower hall toward the stairs when the landlady's door opened. Bozo darted out, grinning a welcome. Then Mrs. Orford, pale-faced, moved toward her.

"Karen, I had to go into your apartment an hour ago. The people below you—you know, the Tillsons—phoned down that water was leaking down around the standpipe in their bathroom. They thought you must have let the basin or bathtub overflow."

"But I'm sure I didn't leave water running!"

"That's right, you didn't. It was the people above you. But the thing is, when I was in your apartment I saw that the wind had shifted and snow was starting to blow in, so I went over to close the window. Karen, somebody broke into your apartment, or tried to. The screen's been cut from the frame all along the bottom and for a few inches up each side."

With the dog scrambling ahead, and Mrs. Orford toiling behind her, Karen hurried up the stairs. Unlocking her apartment door, she switched on the light and then crossed the room. She turned the window latch and slid the sash upward. The screen had been cut, all right. At the center of its lower edge, it bulged outward slightly against the several inches of snow which had accumulated behind it on the window ledge. Karen slid the pane down, locked it.

Mrs. Orford said, "I didn't call the police. I thought you'd want to check first to see what was missing."

Karen nodded. Looking around the room, she saw that her twelve-inch TV still sat on the table at the foot of the studio couch, and her transistor radio was atop the desk. Her only piece of jewelry worth stealing, a platinum watch, was clasped around her wrist, and all the cash she had was in the red bag hanging from her shoulder.

Turning, she looked at the landlady's distressed face. Mrs. Orford's lips, she noted with alarm, looked bluish. "Nothing's gone."

"Just the same, you must report it. Oh, Karen! I blame myself. I ought to have had bars installed at every window that opens onto the fire escape. But I found out it cost hundreds! And what with taxes and all—"

"It's not your fault. I should always lock my window before I go out."

"You really should, dear. Always. And you'll report it to the police?"

"Yes, right away." No need to tell her already upset landlady that she had far more than a cut window screen to report to the police.

When her landlady had gone, Karen stood there for a moment, staring at the window. When had it happened? Not today, certainly. Snow had accumulated, undisturbed, on the outer window ledge. Last night, as she slept? No, she was a light sleeper. Besides, Bozo would have set up an instant alarm. He had strong views about the sacredness of his living quarters. One Saturday the previous fall, when workmen had been repairing the apartment house roof, he'd become quite hysterical at the sight of strange men clambering up and down outside the window. She'd finally had to shut him in the bathroom.

No, it must have happened fairly early the night before, after she'd gone down to see Slide Thompson.

But she'd left Bozo in this apartment when she went down to Times Square. Why had he accepted the intruder quietly, or at least with so little fuss that no one had phoned down to Mrs. Orford?

Hands turning cold, she realized the answer. Bozo had known the person who'd entered this apartment last night.

David. He knew David.

But not only David. He knew, and regarded as friends, the owners of all his playmates on the hill. And with the screening that rotten, any one of them, even May Cosgrove, could have cut the window screen and stepped, with little or no challenge from Bozo, into this darkened room.

Every one of those people, some for reasons unknown to her, had shielded David, and thereby involved themselves in the killing of that old man. Thus she, or anyone who might learn their secret, became a possible source of danger to them.

Again she had a sense of being ringed in by hostile, frightened faces. Now, though, when she knew that it was nothing less than cold-blooded murder which they'd covered up, the feeling was much stronger. As she stood there in the center of the silent room, she felt that if she walked into the darkened bathroom or the darkened kitchen, she might find herself face to face with one of them. Paul Winship, smiling his malicious little smile. May Cosgrove, eyes hidden by the glitter of her glasses. Consuelo Bryant, with her chocolate-brown stare.

Although she knew it was absurd, the feeling was so strong that she had to act upon it. Swiftly she walked to the kitchen, switched on the light. No one. No one in the bathroom either.

But that sense of danger crouched to spring at her persisted. Aware that she trembled, she returned to the living room and jerked the window shade down over the sill. Then she looked at the phone. If she called the police, they might not arrive for a long time, perhaps not even until after Bill got there at seven-thirty. She couldn't wait here alone that long, ears straining for the sound of stealthy movement on the fire escape or in the hall outside her door. Nor could she inflict herself, in her present jittery state, on Mrs. Orford.

Never mind her soaked clothing. Just feed Bozo, leave a note for Bill, and catch a taxi over to the precinct house on Sixty-seventh Street. On the way she'd stop by the kennels. Bill was probably there. He could accompany her to the police.

A taxi? There'd be almost no cabs on Manhattan's snow-clogged streets tonight. No matter. It would take her only fifteen minutes or so to walk those short north-south blocks to the police station.

While Bozo slurped his dinner in the kitchen, she sat down at her desk and wrote, "Had to go out." She hesitated. No, better not to say where. "Will you please ring the manager's apartment?" She signed it, then doubled the note over and wrote "Bill" on the outside.

A few minutes later, holding onto Bozo's leash, she rang Mrs. Orford's bell. When the landlady opened the door, Karen said, "I'm going over to the police station now."

Mrs. Orford frowned. "It's so bad out. Wouldn't it be better to phone?"

"You know how overworked the police are. It might be days before they got around to investigating a little thing like a cut screen. But if I go there and raise a fuss, maybe they'll do something. Anyway, Bozo needs walking."

Before the landlady could object further, Karen rushed on, "But I'm expecting a Mr. Bailey. We have a dinner date. Is it all right to leave a note asking him to ring your apartment? You can tell him where I've gone."

"Of course, dear. And if he wants to, he can wait for you in my apartment."

"Thank you," Karen said. She walked out to the foyer, thrust the note into the little frame that held the name plate beside her bell, and then moved through the still-falling snow down the apartment house steps.

She'd been right not to count on a taxi. Most of the street lay buried, curb to curb, in snow. Only a few cars moved over the clear strip down its center, their snow tires throwing brown slush. Except for a place here and there where snow had been shoveled away, the sidewalk, too, had been reduced to a narrow little canyon between snowbanks at least a foot high. Bozo, who loved snow as much as he hated rain, trotted ahead of her, nose sniffing at the slush, plumy tail waving. When they reached the corner, he tried to continue north, toward his friends on the hill. "No, Bozo," she said. Turning left, she moved toward Bill's street, Eighty-second.

A girl seated behind the desk in Bill's basement office, probably the same girl who'd answered the phone the night before, looked at Karen coolly through horn-rimmed glasses. No, Mr. Bailey wasn't here. He'd gone over to the Brooklyn kennels that morning, and wasn't expected to return to this office.

"Thank you," Karen said. Apparently he intended to come straight from Brooklyn to her apartment. Ascending the areaway steps to the sidewalk, she looked toward Fifth Avenue only a few feet away, with the Metropolitan Museum, dimly visible through the snow curtain, rising on its opposite side.

She might as well go along Fifth, she decided, on the Central Park side of the street. At Seventy-ninth, just south of

164

the museum, there was an entrance to the park. She'd allow Bozo a necessary minute or so among the bushes in there, and then continue on to the police station.

With the gun weighting his overcoat pocket, David Bryant climbed to the apartment house foyer. He reached out to ring the bell before he saw the note, stuck in the name-plate frame. "Bill." Almost surely she'd left it for Bill Bailey, that kennel owner she'd dated. He opened the note, read it, and then, after a moment, took the handkerchief from his breast pocket and spread it over the little intercom grille. Voices sounded pretty much alike over that tinny mechanism, but still, Mrs. Orford knew his voice, and there was no point in taking unnecessary risks.

He rang her bell. Through the linen he'd spread over it, the intercom gave a preliminary squawk. Then Mrs. Orford's voice said tinnily, "Hello."

"Mrs. Orford? This is Bill Bailey."

"Oh, yes. The young man who's taking Karen to dinner. She asked me to tell you, Mr. Bailey, that she had to go over to the police station on Sixty-seventh Street."

Fear closed up his throat. When he could speak, he asked, "Some sort of trouble?"

"Yes. A prowler. We found her window screen cut."

His panic subsided a little. She hadn't confided in her landlady. Maybe she hadn't told anyone else, either. If he could get to her before . . . "How long ago did she leave, Mrs. Orford?"

"Oh, not ten minutes ago." Her next words set his terror leaping again. "She said she was going to drop by your place on the way, but I see she's missed you. Would you like to wait in my apartment for her?"

He was aware of cold sweat on his forehead and upper-lip. If she spilled the whole thing to Bill Bailey, as she doubtless intended to, then the last chance was gone. All he could do was to make a run for it. But if Bailey wasn't there, he still had a chance, although a slim one. The kennel was only a few feet from the corner of Fifth Avenue. After she left Bailey's, she'd probably turn onto Fifth, especially if she had her dog with her.

"Mr. Bailey, are you still there? I asked if you wanted to wait in my apartment."

"No, thank you. I'll just go over to the police station myself. Oh, one thing more. Did she take her dog with her?"

"Yes."

"Well, good night, Mrs. Orford."

Jamming the handkerchief and the note deep into his overcoat pocket, he hurried down the steps and turned north. On the corner stood a red phone booth. The door, its lower edge blocked by snow, for perhaps a half a minute resisted his efforts to open it. Once inside, though, he saw with relief that the phone appeared unvandalized and the Yellow Page directory intact. He looked up the number, fumbled a coin into the slot, dialed. No, a girl's voice told him, Mr. Bailey wasn't in the office, nor expected to be. Hanging up, he left the booth. With snowflakes blinding his eyes, he hurried along a sidewalk that had narrowed to a slushy footpath.

Within minutes after she crossed Fifth Avenue and turned south along the broad new esplanade with its rows of naked-limbed trees, Karen wished that she'd retraced her steps to Madison Avenue. On Madison many of the shops would still be open, spilling light onto pedestrians moving along the snow-narrowed sidewalk. Here there was only the looming façade of the museum, its many windows dark, and, across the wide avenue, the tall apartment houses only dimly visible through the falling snow. At the moment, at least, no cars moved along the avenue, although the opposite curb was lined with ghostly white mounds, each hiding an automobile that might remain entombed for several days.

As for the esplanade along which she moved, evidently

she was the first person to have done so for at least an hour, because the ever-thickening snow lay unbroken in the aisles between the trees. She became aware that in the silence each of her footsteps made an odd sound, a kind of squeaky crunch. After a moment she realized the reason. Her booted feet, sinking deep into the freshly fallen snow, broke through the frozen crust of the old snow at each step. Moving along, with the dog floundering ahead of her and wet snow flakes swirling into her eyes, she began to feel as if she and Bozo were the only living creatures who'd ventured to the fringe of Central Park tonight.

Except for them, of course. At least some of them would be meeting on the hill even tonight, drawn there not because of their dogs or a liking for each other's company, but out of their shared guilt and unease. She thought of them gathered there, with the rays of the standard lamp struggling through the snow curtain to cast a cold greenish light on their dark figures . . .

The Seventy-ninth Street entrance to the park lay just ahead. She crossed the driveway into the museum's south parking lot, and then the double road leading into and out of the park, its white expanse marred by only one set of rapidly disappearing tire tracks. A few yards beyond the curb lay the entrance to one of the park's many footpaths. She'd move a little way down the path, allow Bozo off the leash only as long as necessary, and then hurry down to the lights and the comparatively crowded sidewalks of Madison Avenue.

She'd just reached the other side of the street when she stopped short, her heartbeats suddenly rapid and heavy. One of them was coming toward her. She saw the Airedale take shape through the swirl of snowflakes first, and then the tall, thin figure.

Paul Winship, who by his silence had made himself a party to the ruthless murder of a sick old man. Paul, who might or might not have guessed that she intended to tell the police about that murder.

In another moment they'd be face to face. Feeling mingled revulsion and fear, she turned and, with Bozo struggling ahead of her, moved as rapidly as she could along the path leading into the darkness and silence of the park.

Something seized the strap of her shoulder bag, jerking her to a halt.

After a few paralyzed seconds, she realized that the strap had caught on the branch of a bush projecting out over the path. She was about to turn to free herself when she heard, close behind her, the squeaky crunch of footsteps.

Fear sent her lunging forward. She heard a ripping sound as the remaining stitches that held the strap to the bag gave way, freeing her shoulder. "Hey!" he said. "Hey, Karen."

She didn't turn. Heart racing with panic now, she moved forward as rapidly as she could. Those squeaky footsteps followed. "Hey!" he called again.

Suddenly in snow up to her knees, she knew she must have blundered off the path. No use to try to escape him now. He was close behind her, and his legs were much longer than hers. She turned and said, in a high, shaking voice, "You leave me alone!"

Only a few feet separated them. And yet as he stood there, on the path's slightly higher ground, he was just a blurred, dark shape through the thickly falling snow. "Sweetie," he said, "you've got nothing to worry about. You're not my type, and never were."

Turning, he moved back toward Fifth Avenue.

She stood there, waiting for her heartbeats to slow. After a minute or so she moved back up to the path and unsnapped Bozo's leash. "Be quick about it," she told him.

Following as rapidly as possible the footsteps—Karen's?—that broke the whiteness of the esplanade in front of the museum, David saw Paul Winship moving toward him. Ask

168

Paul about her? Better not. Afterwards, Paul would remember. And yet, if he had seen her . . .

Paul himself solved the dilmema. As both men halted, he said, "Hi, David. What's with your girl friend?"

"Which girl friend?"

"Karen. We were almost face to face at Seventy-ninth Street back there when she bolted into the park like a scared rabbit. She on goof balls or something?"

"I wouldn't know. She and I are all washed up."

Paul's voice lost its jocular tone. "You don't suppose she's hip to something, do you?"

"How could she be? Excuse me, Paul. I've got a date, and I'm late for it."

"Not bringing Britt up to the hill tonight?"

"No." Moving out into the unbroken snow, he walked past the other man. "I took her out for a run earlier."

Paul called after him, "Good luck with the new babe!"

Karen snapped the dog's leash to his collar. Reluctant to leave the park, he hung back for a moment, and then floundered obediently ahead of her, tail waving.

She'd almost reached the bush which had snatched her purse from her when she saw the tall figure, hesitating there beside the standard lamp on Fifth Avenue. Halting, she stood motionless.

Her fear of Paul Winship had proved groundless. But this man was different. This one had killed, and could again. He stood there with his pale hair gleaming through the snow curtain like an angel's. Death angel.

For an unmeasured interval she stood paralyzed, like some small animal awaiting the slash of a fang, the dart of a snake's head. Then, as she realized that she stood in comparative darkness, that perhaps he hadn't seen her, she found that she could move. Turning, she struggled deeper into the park.

Perhaps the falling snow had thinned just then. Perhaps his ear had caught the faint jingle of Bozo's metal collar tags as the dog turned to plow ahead of her. Whatever the reason, she heard the squeak of pursuing footsteps.

23

Even though she had a head start of perhaps a hundred feet, she knew with bleak sureness that her only chance was to keep straight ahead. If she blundered off the walk, if she again found herself floundering through the deeper snow at her left, he would overtake her in no time. But it was hard to keep a sense of direction. Before she'd struggled more than a few yards, the lights on Fifth Avenue had been swallowed up by the falling snow. A standard lamp, somewhere up ahead and to her right, shone through the smother as only a greenish glow.

And yet she was grateful for those flakes that blotted out light, and stung her eyes, and blew into her open, laboriously breathing mouth. It was the thick, swirling snow that hid her from her hunter. She had a cold, sick certainty that without it she'd have felt by now the impact for which her whole body was braced, the bone-and-flesh-shattering impact of a bullet.

One of the park's several hills must be just ahead, a fairly steep hill which, on weekend afternoons in good weather, was bright with colorfully dressed young people playing guitars, and sunbathers, and racing children and dogs. To her now, already half exhausted, the hill would be a deathtrap. Before she'd struggled even a little way up it, those squeaking footsteps would have overtaken her.

Turn right, toward the museum, and then try to double back toward Fifth Avenue? No, he'd expect her to do that. She turned sharply left, praying that she wouldn't find herself floundering in knee-deep snow. Yes, she'd judged right. The snow underfoot, no deeper here, told her that she'd turned onto the intersecting path. After a moment she felt a surge of wild hope. The pace of those squeaking footsteps had slackened. Then the sound ceased entirely, as if he'd paused to try to decide which way she'd gone.

The greenish, snow-diffused halo of a standard lamp ahead. She must avoid the lamp, lest it afford him a dim glimpse of her. And she must rest—rest. Her blood made a seething sound in her ears now, and pain stabbed her right side.

If she remembered correctly, the hill was lower and far less steep along about here, with a little grove of trees halfway up the slope. If she and Bozo could hide there for at least a few minutes, their bodies blending with the dark tree trunks . . .

She turned right, over ground that sloped gently upward. Yes, there were the black, rounded shapes of the low trees. Moving carefully so as not to break branches, she made her way into the grove and then dropped to the snow, her arm around the dog. Puzzled, sensing her fear, he whined faintly. "Quiet," she whispered, and he obeyed

How long could she stay huddled here without danger of freezing to death? She had no idea. And what if David, too, had finally turned to his left, and was moving along the footpath below?

The dog moved closer against her. Should she, if need be, order him to attack? No, even if Bozo understood, which was by no means certain, since he hadn't been trained as an attack dog, David would only shoot him first and then turn the gun on her. What should she do, then, if she saw a dark figure moving toward her up the hill?

The Rambles, she thought. Its entrance was just beyond the other side of this hill.

Once a favorite haunt of lovers and bird-watchers, that hilly wooded area of winding paths known as the Rambles had of late years become a sinister place. Even in the daytime, ordinary citizens seldom ventured into the area except in groups. She herself, the one time she'd gone in there, had been with a Bokarski Films camera crew, assigned to making a documentary on Central Park.

By night, the Rambles became a place of whispering evil. Male homosexuals drifted along the paths between the trees and huge boulders. Muggers haunted the area too, and pushers and drug addicts. Only a woman intent upon meeting death by mass rape would go in there alone after dark.

No, not the Rambles, she thought, even though it offered a hundred hiding places, because despite the cold and the blinding snow, at least a few dark figures, if only desperate, hung-up addicts and their suppliers, might be moving along those tortuous paths . . .

Her heart gave a painful throb. Someone was down there at the foot of the hill, his body taking dim shape in the standard lamp's blurred glow. He halted, and she saw the dim gleam of his pale hair. Then, turning around, he moved out of the diffused light.

Her surge of thanksgiving was brief. Another light down there on the path shone through the swirling snow, a small reddish flame, as if from a cigarette lighter held close to the ground. Almost immediately snow quenched it, but surely not before he'd seen her footprints leading up the hill.

The leash in her hand, she scrambled to her feet. Get to the other side of the hill—get there fast. A branch cracked as, bent double, she emerged at the other side of the grove, but that couldn't be helped. Heart laboring, she struggled up the rest of the slope, started down the other side.

Her toe caught against something. She fell headlong and began to slide. Those rocks, she thought numbly. She'd forgotten there was a long rocky outcrop on this slope. Letting go of the leash, she groped with both hands for something that would check her slide, but found nothing. She landed in snow, with the breath knocked out of her, on what she knew must be one of the automobile roads winding through the park.

After a moment she got to her hands and knees. "Bozo!" she called softly.

No eager whine, no furry shape crowding close to her. Then she saw him, by the diffused glow from a light in the parking lot across the road, lying a few feet from her. She crawled to him.

The dog too, apparently, had lost his footing on the slope. Perhaps her own helplessly sliding body had knocked him onto his side. But he'd been less lucky than she, Her hand, slipping under the side of his head, encountered sticky warmth behind his ear. The rock, she thought numbly. He must have struck some jagged little pinnacle only lightly cushioned by snow. Was he dead? Her frantic hand groped through the fur of his chest. Yes, there was his heartbeat, faint but regular.

It must have been some sixth sense that made her look up. On the crest of the hill, clearly visible now through the thinning snowfall, a man stood. By some trick of perspective, he looked enormously tall. His gaze seemed to be directed, not down toward her, but along the hill's crest.

There was no help for it, she thought despairingly. She couldn't save Bozo by staying here. David would see them soon, and come plunging down the hill and kill them both. She'd have to run for shelter, hoping that he wouldn't try to shoot her from a distance, lest he succeed only in attracting the attention of whatever police were patrolling the park tonight.

She got to her feet and ran, floundering across the road, across the parking lot, toward the dark line of trees that marked the beginning of the Rambles.

In the foyer of Karen's apartment house, Bill Bailey pressed the button beside her name, waited, pressed again, waited, and then, swearing, pressed a third time, leaving his finger on the bell.

24

There was a path entrance somewhere nearby, but Karen didn't stop to look for it. Instead she moved straight in among the trees. The ground here, sloping upward, was uneven beneath the snow. She hadn't taken more than a dozen steps before her right leg sank in above the knee. She withdrew her foot, moved a little to her right, and then continued to climb until a snow-buried rock, rolling underfoot, sent her lurching into a tree trunk. She paused then, rubbing a bruised shoulder and trying to quiet her heavy breathing.

She listened. Nothing. Tonight, with almost no surface traffic moving, even what she thought of as "that New York sound" had been stilled—that low rumble made by the combined sound of countless cars moving above ground and dozens of subway trains moving below. Just silence here, and a few snowflakes sifting down through the trees.

Somewhere below her, a twig snapped.

With her stomach a cold knot of fear, she floundered to the crest of the rising ground and then down through trees on the opposite slope. She could see, just ahead, the ghostly gleam of a snow-covered footpath.

She turned onto it. Then, seeing the greenish glow of a standard lamp ahead, bright through the snowfall that had become fine-flaked and thin, she swerved onto an intersecting path. She followed its winding, down-sloping course for perhaps twenty yards, turned onto another path, and stopped short.

The sound of men's voices, speaking not more than a few yards away. Hushed, furtive voices, punctured by a soft laugh. She saw, or thought she could see, several dim shapes gathered in a pool of shadow under a tree.

Hysteria, wild and unreasoning, welled up in her then. She turned and plunged off the path into the trees. Leafless branches slapped her face and body. Dead twigs of bushes snapped as she blundered into them. Dimly she realized that she was making too much noise—far too much—enough that David would have no trouble in following her. But in her panic she couldn't check her headlong flight. She came to a path and, fearful that God only knew what might be moving along it—mugger, rapist, drug pusher—she floundered across it to the trees on its opposite side. She was hopelessly lost now. Here among the trees and boulders and finely sifting snow, she had no more sense of direction than if she moved through some far-north wilderness. Again and again she collided with trees. Once she stumbled and fell over something that felt like a log. A few seconds after she got to her feet and moved on, she became aware of a sticky warmth running from her left temple down her cheek. I must have hit a rock when I fell, she thought numbly, and wondered why the wound didn't hurt.

Another path ahead. She started to plunge across it and then halted. From the corner of her eye she'd caught a glimpse of something, the dim, looming shape of a peak-roofed building. It must be that little pavilion, open at each end, which she remembered from that day with the camera crew. Inside, benches faced each other along its walls. Apparently tonight none of the Rambles' furtive prowlers had gathered there, because the snow between her and the building lay unbroken.

If she could take shelter in there from the salt-fine snow

and the worst of the cold, if she could lie hidden under one of those benches . . .

She moved up the path, entered the little pavilion. After the snow glimmer outside, its interior seemed pitch-black. But at least the wooden floor was blessedly solid underfoot. Her left hand, groping down, found a wooden surface at about knee height. She lay down and rolled under the bench.

How blessed not to have snow stinging her eyes. How blessed to lie down and hear her sobbing breath become quiet and feel her heartbeats slow. Then, after a minute or so had passed, the wound in her temple began to ache. She wondered dizzily if she were still bleeding, but raising her hand to find out seemed too much of an effort.

The squeak of footsteps outside.

Her breath, even her heartbeats, seemed to stop. Footsteps on the wooden floor now. Uneven steps, one foot coming down hard, the other dragging.

The footsteps ceased. "Karen."

So he'd found her. It had all been for nothing, the floundering through snow, the log tripping her, the wound in her temple . . .

"Karen, I know you're here. I saw your tracks outside."

She thought, with weird detachment, his foot, or probably his ankle—he must have injured it. That was why he hadn't caught up with her until now. But all of the time, or most of it, he must have been close enough behind to hear her blundering progress.

"You're under the bench, aren't you? You might as well come out."

Come out. Try to talk to him. It was all she could do. Otherwise he'd just kneel on the floor, find her with one groping hand, and with the other, the one that must be holding a gun . . .

She said in a voice as mechanical as a doll's, "All right, David."

She rolled from under the bench, got to her hands and knees. A split second after she'd risen shakily to her feet, vertigo assailed her, and she sank down onto the bench.

Her eyes had grown accustomed to the darkness. When her dizziness abated a little, she could see him sitting on the bench opposite her, his body a deeper dark against the dark wooden wall, his hair faintly gleaming.

"David," she asked in that mechanical voice, "have you got a gun?"

His own voice sounded dull. "Yes."

"You mustn't kill me, David. You'll get caught."

He was silent for several seconds. Then he asked. "Who have you told? About Dockweiler, I mean, and why I did it."

Would a lie be wiser, or the truth? It was so hard to think, what with the dizziness and the throbbing in her head. The truth, she decided. If she said she'd told others, he might, in despairing rage, fire that gun—the gun she could see in his hand now, dully gleaming.

"No one but me knows." She paused. "And I won't tell."

"Karen, don't try to make me believe that. You were on your way to the police tonight. Your landlady told me so. Now where is it, the song that Australian wrote?"

So he must have found out, too, that she'd gone to the bookshop. "Mrs. Dockweiler still has it."

"Don't lie. She told me she sold it to you."

"She's the one who lied. Maybe because I told her it was —valuable. She's got it, David."

He sat there silently for a moment. She could feel the fear and despair emanating from him, almost as if it were something tangible.

"I guess you're telling the truth," he said dully. "That means I'll have to find a way of getting it from her, afterwards."

Afterwards. "David," she cried, "you can't kill me. You loved me, didn't you, David?"

"Yes, as much as I could love anyone. But I can't let you ruin everything for me. I killed him to prevent that. I don't want to kill you, Karen, but I've got to."

She saw his hand raise the dully gleaming cylinder. With her back pressing against the wall, trying desperately to break through the solid wood, she whimpered, "No, David, no." Her voice rose high. "Please, David! Don't, don't!"

A dog's bark somewhere on the path. She saw the man opposite her spring to his feet, whirl. Flame spurted, and an explosive sound seemed to rock the little structure.

The dog barked defiantly, closer now. The gun cracked again, and then again.

Scrabble of claws over the wooden floor. And something else. A man's dark shape, in a tackler's crouch, hurtling through the pavilion's doorway. Again the gun fired, but the crouched shape kept coming. She heard the grunting impact of bodies, heard metal—the gun? Yes, surely the gun —strike a wooden surface and slither across it. Then both men were down on the floor.

Somehow she'd gotten to her feet. She stood there, swaying, hearing their labored breaths and the impact of fist against flesh and bone, sensing rather than seeing the grappling, rolling struggle on the floor. The dog, his body pressed against her leg, kept up a hysterical barking.

She heard a grunt of pain. One of the figures rolled free, rose, and staggered out of the pavilion's other doorway, his body blackly silhouetted against the snow glimmer. The other one got to hands and knees and then stood up.

"Karen?" Bill Bailey's voice asked. "You all right, Karen?"

She didn't answer. She had a sense of falling, falling, through black space.

25

Not opening her eyes, she lay there in the comfortable bed knowing that this was a hospital room, knowing, too, that she was awake now, really awake, for the first time in two days. Or was it three?

She'd been fuzzily awake several times during those days. She could remember faces, and even words. A round-faced young doctor saying, "You'll be all right. The head wound isn't bad. Mainly, it's exhaustion and exposure." She remembered a detective—surely he was a detective—with a long Irish face, who asked questions and wrote down her stumbling answers in a looseleaf notebook of black leather. She recalled noticing that the notebook was so old its black leather had worn to grayness where it covered the metal rings.

Bill had been there too, several times, it seemed to her. She remembered how, forehead anxiously creased even as he smiled down at her, he'd told her that Bozo was alive, alive and frisking, in the Bill Bailey kennels.

She opened her eyes. Now and again during the last hazily remembered forty-eight hours or so, she'd had the impression that she was back in the hospital room she'd occupied only days before. But now she saw that this was a quite different room, its walls painted a soft shade of green, its sun-flooded window hung with draperies of a deeper green. Probably it was a different, and newer, hospital than the one to which she'd been taken after David's sudden lurch against her had knocked her to the subway tracks.

David. David was dead. She didn't know who'd told her that, but someone had.

The divided doors opened and a nurse, a pretty red-haired one, poked her head into the room. "Oh! So you're awake."

"Yes," Karen said, and started to sit up.

"Better not." The nurse moved quickly into the room. "Your head, you know."

As the nurse cranked the top portion of the bed frame to form a back rest, Karen reached up and touched the left side of her head. A bandage. But no pain, no throbbing ache and dizziness such as she'd felt as she lay huddled under that bench.

The nurse said, "You have a visitor waiting, a Mr. Bailey. Feel up to seeing him?"

"Oh, yes!"

"I'll tell him," the nurse said, moving toward the door.

The moment he came in, Karen cried, "Oh, Bill! Your eye!"

His left eye, its lid bruised and swollen, was severely bloodshot.

"It'll be okay. Bryant got his thumb in it. That was how he was able to break away." He stood beside the bed, forehead wrinkled and lips smiling. "How do you feel?"

"Not like jogging around the block, but otherwise okay." She paused. "David's dead, isn't he?"

"Yes," Bill said quietly. He drew the visitor's chair close to the bed, sat down. "Maybe he thought I'd find the gun and come after him. Anyway, he ran out onto a steep point of land that juts into Central Park Lake, ducked under the railing there, and tried to make his way down the cliff. He lost his footing, apparently, and fell twenty feet or so to those rocks along the shoreline. He broke his back. He was already dying when the police found him sometime around midnight."

"Did he tell them about—?"

"He knew he was dying. He told them everything."

Icarus, she thought. David was Icarus. His own abilities would have taken him far enough to satisfy most men. But he'd tried to soar even higher on the stolen wings of a dead man's talent.

She said after a moment, "How did you find me?"

"Your dog found you. I just tagged along."

"But how is it you came into the park?"

"Well, I saw that silly red shoulder bag of yours dangling from a bush a little way inside the Seventy-ninth Street entrance—"

"Bill! Before that."

"Well, I went to your place around seven-thirty, just as we'd arranged. You didn't answer your bell. I was sore, damned sore. After all, two nights in a row—Anyway, I finally rang your landlady's apartment and told her over the intercom who I was, and asked her if she knew where you were."

"Did she ask you into her apartment?"

"Yes, and told me about her conversation over the intercom with a guy who'd said he was me. I was certain it was Bryant, and I was almost as certain you'd planned to report more than a slashed window screen to the police."

With a badly upset Mrs. Orford hovering round him, he'd called the precinct house and learned that Karen hadn't been there. He gave her description to the police, received their assurance that they'd search for her, and then set out to look for her himself.

"Your Mrs. Oxford—"

"Orford."

"Anyway, she'd told me you planned to stop by the kennels. I'd forgotten to ask if you'd taken your dog with you, but I figured you probably had, and that meant the chances were you'd turn down Fifth Avenue on the park side of the street."

He'd paused at the Seventy-ninth Street entrance to the park and seen the red shoulder bag dangling from the bush. Sure that something had happened to her, he'd hurried down the walk.

"It had almost stopped snowing by that time. I saw tracks, and I followed them along the base of the hill, and then up to a little grove of trees."

He'd heard it then, the high, despairing yip of a frightened and perhaps injured dog.

"I went over the hill and down the other side. For a minute I thought I was going to slip and break a leg on those damned rocks, but I didn't. I found Bozo floundering around in circles there in the roadway, trailing his leash. That cut behind his ear had stopped bleeding, but he seemed scared and confused. I helped him pull himself together—you know, stroked him and talked to him. Then I picked up his leash and said, 'All right. Find Karen.' He set off at once, nose lowered to some tracks that ran across the road and the parking lot into the Rambles."

Even in the darkness under the trees, even over ground so strewn with rocks and branches that Bill himself would never have been able to follow her trail, Bozo hadn't lost the scent for more than a few seconds at a time. "I'd told him to be quiet about it, and he was. But when he knew he'd almost reached you, it was too much for him. He had to bark."

She reached out her hand, and his big warm hand closed around it. She said, "It was the sight of Paul Winship that frightened me first. I mean, I knew they'd all been shielding David."

"The police know it too, now. They've gotten a complete statement out of each of them."

She thought of quiet, gentle Henry Maize, with that look

184

of long-held anxiety in his eyes. "What will happen to them?"

"Oh, I suppose they'll be indicted, and have to stand trial, all except May Cosgrove. She's balmy as they come. Why—" He broke off, and then said lamely, "She even buried the gun that killed Dockweiler. Under a privet bush in her yard."

He'd been about to mention what the police had learned, both from David Bryant and Mrs. Cosgrove, about the two boxes of candy. But no. He'd wait until she was stronger before he told her that she had indeed almost fed her dog —and herself—marzipan laced with insecticide.

"As for the others, I should think juries would be inclined to go easy. Certainly it's understandable that his sister would want to protect him, especially considering he'd said that he hadn't intended to kill Dockweiler, or anyone. And George Kinsing—well, he'd have gone to the police right away, if it hadn't been for his wife. He holds himself responsible for a nervous breakdown his wife once had, and so he felt he had to go along with her."

"And Henry Maize?"

"He once killed a hitchhiker in a hit-and-run accident, and Bryant knew about it. Maize will have to stand trial for that, probably, as well as the other. How long he'll get not even my friend Frank Rossi can guess. It'll be up to some judge and jury. But I do know that if I were on a jury, I'd take a dim view of Paul Winship. He was the only one who kept quiet out of sheer greed—money-greed and fame-greed."

"You mean, he wanted David to help him with his songs."

Bill nodded. "He had delusions that his last name was McCartney, not Winship."

They sat there in silence for a few moments holding hands. Then Bill said in a strained voice, "I suppose this is no time to talk about the future."

"Whose future?"

"Well, yours and mine. I mean, both the kennels are going pretty well . . ."

His voice trailed off. Karen said, "You're right. A hospital room isn't the most romantic of settings. Just the same, I'd be inclined to accept."

Even his bloodshot eye lit up. "You would?"

"Of course. I'm no fool." She smiled at him tenderly. "Free dog-walking service for the rest of my life. What girl could resist?"